Zoey's Moving On

"Mom," I said, my voice trembling, "when exactly does Zoey have to leave?"

My mom looked at my dad and didn't answer. Dad cleared his throat and put his hand on my arm.

"Zoey leaves right after the party, Molly," he said quietly.

I knew from the expression on Dad's face that this was real. Zoey was going away.

I turned back to face my mother.

"You don't love Zoey," I said, my voice mean. "You don't care what happens to her, do you?"

I saw the awful look on Mom's face, but I kept on talking.

"Well, *I* love her. There has to be a way to stop this, and I'm going to find it. No matter what, I'm not going to let Zoey leave us!"

Keep Your Hands Off My Orangutan!

Zoey & Me

MALLORY TARCHER

Chapter 1

"**W**hat do you mean, Zoey's leaving us?" I hollered. If I didn't have such perfect coordination and self-control, I'd have dropped *both* bowls of Chunky Monkey ice cream instead of just one.

Mom bent down and pushed the blob of ice cream back into its bowl. She wiped her fingers on her jeans—another sign that my entire world was turning upside down right before my eyes—then put the bowl on the coffee table.

"Ssshh!" she warned, putting her finger against her lips and looking over her shoulder as if she suspected someone was listening just outside the living room. "You'll wake her. You know how she hates to miss out on any excitement. If she hears your voice, she'll be down here in a minute."

I couldn't believe my mother was worried about Zoey's waking up when two minutes ago she'd told me Zoey was being taken from us—from *us,* the only family she'd ever known!—to go live in some bogus zoo in Ohio. I mean, let's talk priorities here!

"Uh, as long as you brought me that ice cream, Moll, I think I'll just go ahead and eat it, okay?"

"What?" I whirled, and for the first time since I'd burst into the living room after overhearing—okay, so I eavesdropped—my parents whispering about Zoey's having to leave us because of some zoo exchange program, I looked at my dad. "Yeah, sure," I said and handed him the bowl of melting Chunky Monkey I hadn't dropped.

Dad took the bowl and settled on the edge of the couch, close to my mom. I saw him look from me to her and back again. I could tell he was worried.

I turned back to Mom and in what even I admit was an incredibly whiny voice asked, "But why? Why does she *have* to go? Can't the Los Angeles Zoo just give the Northern Ohio Zoo another animal? Why does it have to be Zoey?"

Mom ran a sticky hand through her red hair and sighed. For the first time, even through my anger and fear and sadness, I noticed that my mom looked—well, not ancient, but old. I mean, for the past three weeks I'd noticed that something was bothering her. So far this week my usually calm and superorganized mother had forgotten to pick Brad up from baseball practice, packed Brad's favorite lunch for me and my favorite lunch for him, and ironed a hole right through my dad's best shirt.

At first, I figured it was just another ordinary crisis at work that was making my mom slightly batty. See, she's a primatologist at the Los Angeles Zoo. That means she works with and takes care of certain kinds of apes. My mom loves her job, and a lot of times it's really fun. But sometimes she's under a lot of pressure. She's got a lot of responsibility at the zoo, both to the animals and to the people who employ her. Add to that Brad, my fifteen-year-old superobnoxious, sports-nut brother; my dad, a pediatrician, who's really a fabulous guy—so fabulous, in fact, that most of my friends have him as their doctor; Zoey, who was just about to turn one year old and was already experiencing the "terrible twos"; and finally, me (though *I'm* never any trouble), and you can see that my mom really is busy.

"Molly," Mom said, "why don't you sit down . . ."

I shook my head and felt my curls fly. Like my mom, I have red hair. All the women in our family do. Even Zoey.

"No, Mom. I don't want to sit. I want to understand what's going on! Why is my baby sister being taken away?"

Mom sighed again and covered her face with her hands. That scared me. Was my mother going to cry?

"Mom?" I said, nervously. "Okay, I'll sit." And I did, practically landing in my father's lap. He scooted over just in time to avoid my butt ending up in his half-empty bowl of Chunky Monkey.

Mom took her hands from her face, and I was relieved to see that she wasn't crying. There's something totally frightening about seeing your parents cry, unless it's because they're happy. Why *do* adults cry when they're happy?

"First, Molly," she said, looking straight at me, "I didn't mean to keep this from you and Brad. You know we don't like secrets in this family. Do you believe me?"

Mom still looked so sad, I didn't think *I* could answer without crying, so I nodded instead.

"Good. The other thing you should know is that for the past three weeks I've been trying desperately to get this decision reversed, to find some loophole or way out of the agreement."

Mom paused, and I said, "So that's why you've been so distracted lately."

Mom raised her eyebrows. "Have I? I didn't even notice." Then she smiled. "I guess that means you're right."

I knew Mom was trying to make me smile, too, but I just couldn't. Mom must have realized that, because she continued to talk.

"Let me explain the situation, Molly, so you'll know what I've been up against."

I sat up straight and tried to pay attention. I wanted to know everything about what was happening to Zoey.

"There's a program called the Species Survival Plan," Mom began. "SSP. The plan targets about two hundred different types of animals. About seventy-two species are managed for breeding purposes. One of those is the orangutan. Each species is appointed someone called a stud keeper, or species coordinator, who tells zoos when and where and whom to breed."

"Why?" I asked.

"Because that way the species achieves as much genetic diversity as possible with whatever number of animals are available for breeding," Mom explained.

Genetic diversity means "coming from different parents." I only know this because my parents are always using science words. I have to look them up so I can figure out what they're saying!

"Zoos play an important part in protecting endangered species, Molly," my dad added. "And one way they do it is by breeding so that there are more and healthier members of the species born each year."

Mom now squatted on the floor in front of me. "I know it's hard to accept, Molly," she said, looking straight into my eyes, "but the intention is to help Zoey and other orangutans, not to hurt them. What happened was this. Zoey's grandmother, Lucy, Lucky's mother, was traded to the Los Angeles Zoo from the Northern Ohio Zoo, for breeding purposes. The deal was that Lucy's first grandchild would be traded back to the Northern Ohio Zoo for breeding. Zoey is that grandchild."

I thought I saw a bright spot of hope. "But Zoey's not ready for breeding yet, Mom," I pointed out. "She's just a baby."

Mom smiled, but the smile didn't reach her eyes. "That's true, Molly," she said, standing from her crouch. "But the deal was that the Northern Ohio Zoo would take the grandchild when he or she was still young enough to fit into the zoo's orangutan population. Let's face it," Mom said with a shrug, "Zoey doesn't know much about other orangutans. She acts like an orangutan because of her genetic makeup, because she *is* an orangutan. But almost everything she's *learned* since she was born has been about the human world."

The more Mom told me about the zoo exchange program and how it helps endangered species stay alive and get stronger, the more it seemed like Zoey was going to be leaving us forever and there was nothing we could do about it.

Suddenly, another horrible thought occurred to me. Mom was saying something about the Northern Ohio Zoo, but I spoke right over her. "What about Zoey's birthday party?" I cried. "We've been planning it for so long, and everyone's invited already!"

It was true. Zoey was turning one in a few days, and we were hosting a big party at our house for her. Mom was making a new party dress for Zoey. She let me pick out the color. I chose purple.

Brad and I were teaching her how to play games for the party. We started with hide-and-seek. Orangutans have excellent memories for time and place and in the wild use these abilities to find food. In the Miles house, though, these skills were not serving Zoey well at all. She was really great at hiding and never coming out, but really bad at seeking. The minute Brad or I would leave the room to hide, Zoey would lose interest and look for something to swing from. One day she hid so well it took Brad and me almost an hour to find her. We were scared we'd lost her and convinced Mom would kill us if we had. But we finally found her sleeping in the bottom of my closet.

Anyway, Dad had invited his patients who were

celebrating their first birthdays, too—and their moms and dads, of course. The idea still makes me roll my eyes. A house full of one-year-olds, led by a big hairy one who was into hanging from the chandelier! And I'd invited my entire class—even Freddie Finkle, whom I used to hate but then decided I liked when he called Margie Lussman, the girl I hate whom Zoey hates, a wimp. Freddie was bringing some food for the party. "I'll get my mom to bake something," he had said. "What do orangutans eat, anyway? Peanut butter or chocolate chip cookies?"

I'd even invited my teacher, Mrs. Hurwitz, who really liked Zoey in spite of the time I brought her to class for current events and the time Zoey got involved in the Art Walk. But I'll tell you those stories some other time.

Mom sighed. "Well," she said, "the zoo's festivities will go on as planned. And so will our party. We owe that much to Zoey."

I jumped up. I couldn't stand to sit still any longer, especially not when the next question I had to ask was so painful.

"Mom," I said, my voice trembling, "when exactly does Zoey have to leave?"

My mom looked at my dad and didn't answer. Dad cleared his throat and put his hand on my arm.

"Zoey leaves right after the party, Molly," he said quietly.

I couldn't believe my ears. I thought to myself, This can't be happening. This is a really bad dream, like that one I had after eating eight slices of pepperoni pizza last summer.

I knew from the expression on Dad's face that this wasn't a dream. This was real. It was happening. Zoey was going away.

I turned back to face my mother then and said a terrible thing. Even as I said it, I knew it wasn't true and that I should just shut my mouth. My mouth had gotten me in enough trouble in my twelve years, and you'd think I'd know better. But I don't, and I didn't.

"You don't love Zoey," I said, my voice mean. "You don't care what happens to her, do you?"

I saw the awful look on Mom's face, but I kept on talking.

"Well, *I* love her. There has to be a way to stop this, and I'm going to find it. No matter what, I'm not going to let Zoey leave us!"

And with that, I ran upstairs and headed straight for my room and the comfort of the phone.

I dialed the number of my best friend, Tyler Matthews. Tyler lives just next door. I could have yelled out my window for him, like I sometimes do, but I wasn't in the mood for yelling. Suddenly, all I felt like doing was crying on the shoulder of the one person who would really understand what I was going through.

His phone rang. And rang.

I slammed the phone down and buried my face in my pillow. Tyler wasn't home. I was alone.

Chapter 2

I guess I'd better start at the beginning. By now you've figured out that Zoey, my baby sister, is an orangutan. It's not as weird as it seems. Remember, my mom's a primatologist with the Los Angeles Zoo. Just about a year ago, one of the adult orangutans, named Lucky, gave birth to Zoey. But even though Zoey was incredibly cute—and Brad and Tyler and I were at the infirmary the night she was born, so we know—Lucky didn't understand how to be a mother. My mom explained to us that sometimes, when an animal grows up in captivity, it doesn't develop some basic behaviors it would learn easily in the wild. If Lucky had grown up in the rain forest of Sumatra, she would have watched orangutan mothers with their babies and known how to act when she became a mother. But Lucky didn't grow up in Sumatra. She grew up in a zoo, and when Zoey was born, she kind of freaked.

So the next thing we knew, the Miles family—that's us—adopted Zoey and she became Brad's and my baby sister. Orangutans are a lot like human beings, because they take really good care of their babies. An infant orangutan stays with its mother, sleeping in her nest and riding on her body, for as long as three years, or until the mother has another baby. Having Zoey around was just like having a human baby in the house.

And you know what *that* means. Smelly diapers. Wrecked homework assignments. Baby food on the walls. Mom and Dad having no time for me and Brad anymore. You get the picture. I'm embarrassed to admit it now, but for a while I was pretty jealous of Zoey and all the attention she got. Before she came to live with us, I'd been the youngest kid. Becoming a big sister overnight was tough.

It didn't take long for me to find out that being a big sister is also pretty cool. Zoey relies on me to keep her safe, and I feel totally protective of her. I can't believe I ever wished Zoey hadn't come to live with us. Sure, sometimes she still drives me crazy, like the time she decided to swing from a mobile I'd made in art class and hung from the ceiling fan over my bed. I really liked that mobile.

Being a *little* sister isn't so bad anymore either. Brad is becoming human. Slowly, in the past months, I'd discovered we could be in the same room for almost five minutes before he gave me a nuggie and called me "Red" or a worse name. I've never deserved any of his nuggies or names. I am a perfect sister. I guess he's starting to figure that out, because I recently turned twelve and Brad even gave me a birthday gift: my very own video of *Dirty Harry,* starring Clint Eastwood. He's my total hero. I know, I know, it's kind of weird for a twelve-year-old girl to be into Clint Eastwood movies, but I am, okay?

Mom and Dad gave me the coolest present—a laptop computer with an Internet and e-mail connection! They totally trust me to use it responsibly and not give out my real name or agree to meet with some weirdo or look up pictures of things I'm not even supposed to know about yet. Just about the time Mom and Dad dropped the bombshell about Zoey's going away, Tyler had begun to help me get on the Net.

Did I mention that Tyler has thick blond hair and blue eyes and is actually kind of cute? Lots of girls in our class flirt with him, but I don't. He's my best friend, and I've never thought of him as a *boy*friend. But lately—only sometimes—when we're together, I get a funny twinge in the pit of my stomach and I start staring at a piece of his hair or a freckle on his cheek or something equally embarrassing. When I snap out of it, I'm totally mortified and sure he knows I've been acting goopy, but so far he hasn't said anything to me about my weird behavior. He's a real friend.

But since I'd started having feelings about Tyler, I'd begun to wish I had a really close *girl*friend, someone I could talk to about Tyler. And other stuff.

So life was great—until I decided to be nice and bring my parents some ice cream one night. That's when I overheard them talking about Zoey being transferred to the Northern Ohio Zoo.

Overnight, the birthday party I'd looked forward to became the thing I dreaded—Zoey's going-away party.

Chapter 3

"You're doing it wrong!"

Brad yanked the string from my hand.

"Ow!" I stuck my fingers in my mouth. "That hurt." I pulled them out again and looked at the small red streaks. "I am not doing it wrong," I cried and tried to grab the string back from my brother.

It was the morning after Mom and Dad told me and Brad about Zoey's leaving. We were sitting on the floor in the living room, party paraphernalia strewn all around us. Bags of bright balloons. A piñata. A Pin-the-Tail-on-the-Human poster. (I, by the way, was the human. Brad had taken a picture of me bending over. At first I was angry, but then I got the brilliant idea of blowing up the photo and using it for Zoey's party.)

We were arguing about the knots in the string that would attach the piñata to the chandelier. How lame can you get?

But life in our house was different now. Take the night before. I'd been too upset to sleep, so I'd knocked on Brad's bedroom door. I don't like to go in there. There are things growing in there. But I was desperate.

"Do you know about Zoey?" I'd asked, flipping on

the light without bothering to see if he was awake.

He was sitting up, staring at the ceiling.

"Yeah," he said. "Mom and Dad told me after you ran upstairs."

"So what are we going to do about it?" I asked.

Brad flopped back onto his pillow. "There's nothing to do," he said around a yawn. "It's a done deal. Mom tried everything she could. Everyone at the zoo did."

I couldn't believe it. How could Brad be so calm about Zoey's leaving?

"Don't *you* care, either?" I asked.

Then Brad sat up again and looked me straight in the eye. "Of course I care," he said. "But I don't want to get my hopes up. What's the point?"

Now, as we sat in the living room arguing over a piece of string, it occurred to me that in less than a week Brad would be the only sibling I had left. Maybe I'd better be nice to him.

"I'm sorry, Brad," I said.

Brad looked at me as if I'd suddenly sprouted a big green head.

"For what?" he asked, eyes narrowing.

"For doing the knot wrong," I answered, proud of myself for being so mature.

Brad snorted. "Why should you be sorry? I was the one who pulled the string out of your hands. I should be sorry."

Now who was the mature one?

"I'm just really upset about Zoey," I said.

Brad dropped the string into his lap. "Yeah, me too,"

he admitted. "I couldn't sleep last night. I kept thinking about what it's been like living with her for a year. You know, I can't remember what life was like before Zoey."

"Neither can I," I said. "Do you really think there's nothing we can do?" I asked, hoping that somehow, overnight, Brad had changed his mind.

But he hadn't. "Face it, Moll," he said. "We're kids. There's not much we can ever do."

What could I say to that? Suddenly, the bright party decorations seemed totally out of place. I wanted to shove them all into the trash.

"Here," Brad said. "You make the knot."

Tyler came over before dinner to hang out. I looked up from the magazine I was half-reading to see him crawling through my bedroom window. This is the way Tyler usually comes in. He almost never enters through the back door.

"Hey," he said, when he'd untangled his limbs and stood up.

"Hey," I mumbled. I was depressed. It was looking more and more like there was nothing I could do to save Zoey from losing the family who loved her.

"What's wrong?" Tyler asked as he flopped down on the floor next to me. Tyler knows me very well.

I gave a big sigh and shrugged. "Nothing. Except that Zoey is being traded to a zoo in Ohio the morning after her birthday party and you weren't home last night when I called and I really needed to talk to you . . ."

"What?!" Tyler yelled so loud I cringed.

"Hey, I need these ears!" I shouted back.

He pulled the magazine from my hand and tossed it across the room. "Start at the beginning."

Which I did. I explained all I knew about the Species Survival Plan. I explained how Zoey's grandmother, Lucy, had been traded to the Los Angeles Zoo with the promise that her first grandchild would be traded back. And I told him how miserable I was and how I wanted to stop the trade but didn't know how.

Tyler shook his head. "That doesn't sound like the Molly I know," he said. "Where's your fighting spirit?"

I raised one eyebrow, a trick I'm very proud of being able to perform. "What am I, a cheerleader?"

"No, you're just not a person who gives up easily," he replied matter-of-factly.

Tyler was right. Ordinarily, I'll do whatever it takes to get something I really want.

"Well," I said, "this is different. This time, I'd be fighting the system."

Tyler snorted, something he does particularly well.

"So? Look, are we agreed we can't let Zoey leave?"

I looked at him then and had a split-second goopy.

"I didn't know you cared," I said. "About Zoey, I mean," I added quickly.

Tyler looked at me as if I was very, very slow. "I was there the night she was born, wasn't I?"

"Yes, you were," I agreed.

"Okay." Tyler jumped to his feet and walked over to my messy desk. He shook his head. "Moll, you've really got to throw stuff away sometimes."

I shrugged and followed him. "Whatever. What are you going to do?"

"What *we* are going to do is get on the Net," Tyler explained, as he sat in my desk chair, flipped open my computer, and started connecting to the Internet.

I pulled a low, rickety stool over to the desk. "And then what?" I asked, peering at the computer screen.

Tyler pushed a lock of hair from his eyes. "And then we're going to do a little investigating. What's the name of the zoo Zoey's being transferred to?"

"Northern Ohio Zoo," I replied. "NO Zoo."

Tyler looked at me. "What?"

"NO Zoo. I made that up."

For a second he looked baffled. Then he said "Oh," and turned back to the computer.

"Why are we investigating the NO Zoo?" I asked. "What are we hoping to find?"

"Anything that might help us," Tyler said. "We'll look for articles published about the zoo since Zoey's grandmother was traded. We'll look for anything that might sound negative about the zoo's conditions. Anything that might help us fight the transfer."

I stared at Tyler's left ear and felt another major goopy session coming on. I'd never seen him like this. In charge. Determined. Masterful.

Masterful? Where'd I get that one? I shook myself and fell off the stool.

Tyler looked down at me, sprawled on the floor. "Are you okay?" he asked patiently.

I scrambled to my feet, righted the stool, and sat

down again. "Just fine." If you count humiliated as fine, I thought.

"Okay," Tyler said. He was hooked in. "I'm going to do a search, starting with 'zoos.' Then we'll look under 'orangutans' and 'endangered species'—basically any topic related to Zoey's situation. Ready?"

An hour later, I knew more about orangutans and the SSP than I'd ever thought there was to know. It's amazing how much cool stuff you can find on the Internet.

I also knew a lot more about the Northern Ohio Zoo, which was located in a small town called Greenfield, Ohio. None of it was good. Tyler and I discovered that back when Zoey's grandmother was traded, the zoo was highly rated and well respected. It met all of the goals a good zoo should meet. It provided conservation, education, scientific study, and recreation. Most important, it provided companionship for all the animals, something called mental enrichment and stimulation (especially important for primates, like Zoey), and a place for the animals to go when they didn't feel like being gawked at by crowds of obnoxious people.

Impressive, huh? Tyler and I also learned that in order to be accredited—that means approved—by the American Zoo and Aquarium Association, a zoo must meet a lot of requirements and standards.

But the articles we found also said that, in the last ten years or so, the Northern Ohio Zoo had gone way downhill. In fact, it was a mess. Professional zoo-type people had protested its conditions. Some of its funding had been taken away. Several animals had mysteriously died. Someone had accused the zoo of neglect. The list went on.

"I don't get it," I cried. "If the zoo is so crummy, why is it allowed to stay open?"

Tyler shook his head. "What I don't get is how the Los Angeles Zoo can allow Zoey to go there. They've got to know about the rumors."

Suddenly, my heart sank right into the pit of my stomach. I'm not just saying that. It did.

"My *mother* must know what the NO Zoo is like," I said. "How could she . . ."

I couldn't go on. I really thought I was going to cry.

Tyler patted my shoulder. "Don't jump to conclusions, Molly," he said. "Your mom is great. I'm sure she's done everything she can to keep Zoey here. You believe that, don't you?"

I didn't answer.

"*Don't* you?"

I sighed. "Yeah, I guess I do. I know Mom loves Zoey as much as I do. Maybe more."

I hadn't really thought about how hard Zoey's transfer was going to be for my mom. I mean, Zoey is her baby. She helped her be born. When Mom and Dad had told me about Zoey's transfer, all I thought of was how bad it was going to be for me. And I hadn't even apologized to Mom for accusing her of not loving Zoey.

"Earth to Molly."

"What?" I squirmed on my stool. I'd apologize to Mom the first chance I got. "Oh. Okay, what's next?" I asked.

Just then, the doorbell screamed. Really. That's what it sounded like. Tyler and I jumped.

"What was that?" Tyler asked. "I never heard your doorbell sound like that before."

It screamed again. "Okay, okay, already," I mumbled as I got up. "You keep working," I said to Tyler. "I'll answer the door."

Tyler nodded. "Tell whoever it is to lighten up." He winced as the person on my front doorstep pushed the bell in a new and particularly annoying way. "Go!"

I hurried out of my room and across the landing. Not even the thundering of my feet on the wooden stairs could drown out the insistent screaming of the bell. "Uuurrggghhhh! I'm coming!" I shouted at the closed front door.

I reached the door and, without stopping for a breath, flung it open.

When I saw who—what—stood there, I couldn't decide whether to scream very, very loudly or laugh hysterically. A noise like a grunt but also like a gurgle came out of my mouth.

I stood face-to-face with the scariest-looking woman I'd ever seen.

"Well, child," the woman said, her long, thin lips stretching into a long, thin smile, "aren't you going to invite me in?"

Chapter 4

"**W**hy would I want to do that?"

That's what I thought.

What I said was, "My parents told me not to let strangers in the house. Who are you?"

I'll admit I was a bit rude, but this woman really gave me the creeps. She was tall and very skinny. Not thin. *Skinny*. Her black hair—it was *definitely* dyed—was pulled tightly into a bun, so tightly I could see where the skin around her temples was strained. Gross.

Then there was her nose. It was long, but lots of people have long noses. You should see my dad's. It was what she was doing with her nose that totally weirded me out. She was flaring her nostrils, over and over again, as if she couldn't breathe without doing it. Was it some kind of nostril-toning exercise? Ugh.

Her eyebrows had been plucked out, then drawn on with a black pencil. They looked like spider legs. Her lips—those thin, long lips—were painted with red-red lipstick. We're talking five-alarm fire here. All that was missing were two big circles of blush—one on each cheek. But she wasn't wearing any blush that I could see. Her skin was so pale it looked like she'd dumped

24

an entire container of baby powder on her face.

As if her face wasn't enough to spook me, her clothes made me completely mental.

Her coat was leopard skin, complete with spots. The leopard is an endangered species, and it's illegal to kill a member of an endangered species, especially to make a coat or a pair of shoes out of it. Maybe it's fake, I thought. A lot of other things on her are fake. Maybe this is, too.

But although I'd never seen a live leopard up close and personal—I'd always been safely on the other side of a cage—something told me that this coat was made from what once had been a live leopard. Maybe it belonged to her grandmother, I thought, trying not to assume the worst about this strange woman.

Another gurgle-grunt came out of my mouth just then, as I noticed the scarf around her neck.

It was made from the body of a small animal, or maybe the bodies of several super-small animals. I was too grossed out to look *that* closely. There were no bones or muscles or anything else that goes inside an animal. There was only skin and fur and a head with glassy little eyes. I stared at the eyes and wondered if they were marbles or beads. . . .

Ugh. Even now, thinking about that . . . thing around her neck, I feel like I'm going to barf.

But the very worst part of it all was that she carried a suitcase.

I guess my standing there with my mouth open annoyed the woman, because suddenly she took a big step forward and said, "I'm Ms. Davita. Ms. Lolita Davita, Director of the Northern Ohio Zoo. I'm here for Zoey."

At that moment I had an overwhelming urge to slam the door in her face, grab Zoey, and run off screaming. No way was I going to let this bizarre woman walk off with my baby sister!

Just as I was reaching for the door, I heard Mom's voice from the hall behind me. Rats.

"Ms. Davita, welcome. You're here early."

I stepped aside as my mother greeted Ms. Davita and offered to take her bag. My mother's no weakling—she lugs around primates all day long!—but when Ms. Davita handed Mom her suitcase, Mom almost collapsed. What did she have in there? Probably her makeup, I thought nastily.

My mother recovered quickly and said, her voice and smile a little less bright now, "Two days early, in fact." Mom always makes her point, but in the nicest way.

Before Ms. Davita could answer—or maybe she had no intention of answering—her nostrils gave three huge flares, and before I could duck, she sneezed.

Now, I'm not obsessed with grossness the way lots of kids are, but I enjoy a good gross-out as much as the next person. Let me tell you that when this woman sneezed, it was like getting hit by a killer wave at the beach. My ears started ringing from the impact. It was cool.

Wiping her face as discreetly as possible, my mother looked at Ms. Davita and said, "Bless you."

"Do you want a tissue?" I asked sweetly.

Ms. Davita looked at me as if I were a piece of toenail

fungus and said, her lips curling, "Whatever for?"

Clearly sensing disaster in the form of a really nasty comment from me, my mom took Ms. Davita's elbow and guided her inside.

"Molly," she said, giving me that significant look mothers give you when they're warning you to keep your mouth shut and be good, "please close the door."

I gave my mother the angelic "Who, me?" look kids give their mothers in return and closed the door.

"I guess I'll go upstairs and move my stuff out of my room now," I said, attempting a significant, guilt-producing look of my own at Ms. Davita. "I wasn't ready for you. You're two days early, you know."

"Molly." That's all Mom needed to say. Funny how you can be afraid of your own name.

"See you later," I said and ran back upstairs.

"Who was it?" Tyler asked as I burst into the room He didn't even turn away from the computer.

"How'd you know it was me?" I asked.

"Because it's not likely a herd of water buffalo would be pounding up the staircase," he answered.

"Hmmph." I stood taller and tried to walk across the room like a ballerina, toes pointed out, head held high. "Whoa!"

I tripped over the magazine Tyler had tossed across the room and fell into his back. "Sorry," I mumbled.

He didn't seem to notice. "There. Look, Moll," he said, pointing to the screen. "What do you think?"

I squinted at the screen, and although I could read the words printed there, I wasn't sure what they meant.

"I'm not sure what I'm looking at, Tyler," I complained. "Want to fill me in?"

"Sure," he said pleasantly. "While you were gone, I found an e-mail pen pal service for you to join. I pretended to be you and wrote a description of the sort of person you want to be pals with—"

"Wait a minute," I said, sitting down on the rickety stool. "What does having an e-mail pen pal have to do with helping Zoey?" Before he could respond, I added, "And who gave you permission to pretend to be me?"

Tyler smiled. "I said I was going to help you keep Zoey here, right? And you trust me because I'm your best friend, right?"

"Okay, okay," I grumbled. "Tell me what it's all about."

"So this is what I figured," he went on. "Let's say we can't stop Zoey's actually going to NO Zoo. Wait, don't interrupt," he added as I opened my mouth to protest. "It may take us a while to figure out a really good plan, and we don't have a while. We have only two days. How are we going to keep track of Zoey from here, once she's in Ohio? We don't trust the NO Zoo, right?"

I nodded. "Right."

"What we need is a connection, a spy, someone on the outside who can infiltrate the Zoo and keep an eye on Zoey for us."

Tyler's eyes had gotten all shiny as he spoke.

"You're really into this spy stuff, aren't you?" I asked.

Tyler frowned. "Are you with me or not?"

I sighed. "I'm with you."

"Okay. I figured we should hook up with someone

about our own age who lives close enough to the zoo so he or she can get there easily. The person has to love animals and also has to agree to keep our plan a secret—"

"What plan?" I asked.

"Whatever plan we come up with," Tyler explained. "Sheesh. Anyway, I put your—our—notice up on the board, and now all we have to do is wait for someone to respond. Cool, huh?"

I had to admit, it was a pretty good plan. If Zoey had to go to the NO Zoo for a while, we'd need someone to keep a close eye on her. And that someone should be a kid, like us. Preferably a girl about my own age. I really missed having a girlfriend. The last girl I'd been good friends with, Cyndie Barnes, had moved out of the neighborhood three years ago. We'd written letters back and forth for about six months, until she told me she'd found a new friend and didn't need to write to me anymore.

I'll say this much for Tyler. He's loyal.

"Yeah, it's a good plan, Tyler," I agreed. "I just hope someone normal wants to be my e-mail pen pal. What if some weirdo responds?" I had a momentary flash of some drooling guy in a baseball cap with moose antlers on top sneaking around my backyard, looking for a way into my house.

"Don't worry," Tyler assured me. "This pen pal e-mail is run by a really respected youth service. They do background checks on everyone who writes in. And all correspondence goes through the service before it's sent on to the pen pal. If it's something weird, the service contacts the sender."

"I don't think I want to know any more," I said. "I feel totally exposed already."

"Just leave this part to me," Tyler said. "By the way, you didn't tell me who was at the door."

Now it was my turn to impress. "Just Ms. Lolita Davita," I said casually. "Of the Northern Ohio Zoo. She's staying with us for a few days, you know. And when she leaves, she's taking Zoey with her."

An hour later dinner was ready, and I was exhausted. After Tyler had gone home, I started moving my stuff to Zoey's room—I was going to share with Zoey while Ms. Davita stayed with us—but Zoey had other plans. Every time I brought something into her room, like a pile of clothes, she'd follow me into the hallway and dump them. I'd come back a few minutes later with an armful of books, only to find the last load of stuff heaped outside her door. Nobody can tell me that animals aren't smart. Zoey knew something bad was happening, and she was having none of it.

When Mom called us down for dinner, I kicked the last of my stuff into Zoey's room and slammed the door before she could dash inside to get it.

"Come on, Zoey," I said, taking her hand. "It's time to meet the nice lady from the zoo."

Zoey looked up at me. For a moment, I thought I saw a gleam in her eye. Then she stuck out her long, black, spotted tongue.

"Hey, I feel the same way," I said, giving Zoey's hand a squeeze. "Let's go."

When we walked into the dining room, everybody else was already seated. Mom. Dad. Brad. Ms. Davita. Zoey's high chair stood midway between Ms. Davita's chair and mine.

"Sorry we're late," I said, lifting Zoey in her chair and slipping into my own seat. "Zoey was having fun playing toss with my stuff."

Dad laughed. Ms. Davita did not. Instead, her nostrils flared, and before I could help myself I muttered, "Thar she blows." I don't think anyone heard me, though.

"Well, at the Northern Ohio Zoo," Ms. Davita said, "we value a well-trained animal. I can see we're going to have our hands full with Zoey. We must make up for her lack of training so far."

I shot a look at my mother, whose face was a curious shade of pink. Maybe my mother was the one who was going to blow.

"I think you'll find that Zoey is very well-trained, Ms. Davita," Mom said calmly. "If she's a little rambunctious this evening, it's probably because she's not used to having a new person in the house."

At this very moment, Zoey was piling her spaghetti on her head, one strand at a time.

"Zoey," I whispered. "Don't do that."

Ms. Davita's long, thin lips compressed into a long, thin line, and she poked her fork into her own pile of spaghetti with disdain.

Did I mention she was wearing a tiger-print dress and earrings that I could swear were made of whale bone? Ick.

No one said anything for a few minutes. The only sounds were forks and knives clattering against dishes and Zoey's noisy chewing. I kept an eye on Ms. Davita and saw that she didn't look at Zoey even once. And not once so far had she spoken to her. Strange.

The mistake I made was in paying attention to my own plate for a second too long. I like spaghetti. That's my excuse.

A high-pitched shriek made me drop my fork and jump from my seat. Brad, Dad, and Mom each had the same reaction.

"What in . . ." Dad began. Then, as he looked at Ms. Davita, his mouth fell open.

Zoey was chuckling. While we'd all been concentrating on eating, she'd dumped her entire plate of food on Ms. Davita's head. It was not a pretty sight.

"Oh, Ms. Davita, I'm so sorry," Mom cried, hurrying around the table with a napkin. It's going to take a lot more than one napkin to clean up *this* mess, I thought.

"Bad girl, Zoey," Brad scolded, but gently. He began to wipe red sauce from Zoey's already red head.

Finally, Ms. Davita spoke. "Look," she said, her voice cold and mean, "look what that . . . that . . . that *monkey* did to me!"

She made "monkey" sound like a four-letter word. The bad kind.

"She's not a monkey," I blurted.

"Molly, be quiet," Mom scolded, as she tried to blot Ms. Davita's face.

"But, Mom," I protested. "Zoey's an orangutan, not a monkey. She should know that!"

"Molly!" Dad said, his voice harsh. "Not now."

I stood there, trembling with anger. Who was this woman, anyway? And how dare she call my baby sister a monkey!

Late that night, after everyone had gone to bed, I crept downstairs with my *Dirty Harry* video. I knew Mom would kill me for being up so late on a school night, but I couldn't sleep. I settled in front of the TV with a bowl of Cookies and Cream ice cream (my personal favorite), and with the sound really low so I wouldn't wake anyone up, I watched Clint Eastwood get the bad guys.

Clint made everything look so simple, I thought. You're a bad guy? Pow, you're history.

I pictured myself face-to-face with Ms. Davita. We were alone. Maybe in the kitchen. I couldn't see myself with a real weapon, so I imagined I was holding a . . . whisk. It was the first thing I could think of.

"Go ahead," I said to my enemy. "Make my day."

And then I proceeded to whisk her.

Chapter 5

I slept pretty badly that night. When I'd finished watching *Dirty Harry*, I went upstairs and stood beside Zoey's crib, watching her sleep. But that made me feel too sad, so I lay down on my sleeping bag and stared at the ceiling. Eventually, visions of Zoey being miserable in her new home faded away, and I slept. In my dreams, Zoey found lots of wonderful orangutan friends and was surrounded by zoo personnel who really loved her. Just as Zoey was greeting a crowd of admirers, a bouquet of roses in her arms—which, by the way, she was trying to eat—I woke up.

Don't let anyone tell you that dreams are omens. After I got Zoey dressed—which required only minimal wrestling that morning—I put her back in her crib. "Now stay there while I get dressed, okay?" I said.

Zoey smiled a toothy orangutan smile, and I raced into the bathroom. When I got back, no more than three minutes later, Zoey was gone. After a quick search upstairs—during which I accidentally got a peek at Brad in his underwear—I gave up and went downstairs for breakfast. Mom probably has her, I thought.

Ms. Davita was sitting at the breakfast table. Great.

Why couldn't she have decided to sleep late?

"Good morning," I said. See? I *am* nice.

Ms. Davita nodded in my general direction and took a sip of her coffee.

Where was everyone, anyway? I tried again. "Did you sleep well?" I asked.

Ms. Davita flared her nostrils and said, "Absolutely not. My allergies drove me crazy." She pulled a wad of tissues from her lap and honked into it.

I swallowed hard. The wad looked pretty used. "Oh," I said. "What are you allergic to?"

For a moment Ms. Davita looked stunned, like I'd asked her to reveal some horrible secret. She lowered the soggy wad of tissues and, without meeting my eyes, said, "Just things in general. Dust. Pollen. The air."

"Oh," I said. What else could I say?

Luckily, Brad came bounding into the kitchen just then and, with a nod to the two of us, grabbed three bananas and bounded out. Guess he hadn't seen me seeing him in his underwear.

"Good morning, Ms. Davita. Molly."

Saved by Dad! He took a seat and began to pour himself some coffee.

"Has anyone seen Zoey?"

It was Mom standing in the doorway. Oh, no, I thought. Not again.

Dad frowned. "Molly, have you and Brad been playing hide-and-seek with Zoey again?" he asked.

"No," I answered. My stomach felt queasy. "I thought Mom had brought her down for breakfast."

As if on cue, Zoey swung into the kitchen.

I couldn't help it. I didn't even try. I burst out laughing.

On her head, Zoey was wearing what had to be Ms. Davita's girdle. No way did my mother own something that weird-looking.

"Zoey!" Mom and Dad yelled at the same time. Then, at the same time, they grinned.

Ms. Davita said nothing. She did not grin.

Mom reached for Zoey, but Zoey scooted away. I'd never seen her so disobedient. Clearly, she was performing for Ms. Davita, because, in the next moment, she jumped smack into the zoo director's lap!

"Oh, get it off me!" Ms. Davita screeched, trying to back away but trapped by her chair.

Dad's face became dark, and he plucked Zoey from Ms. Davita's lap. Zoey buried her face in his neck.

"She's sorry, Ms. Davita," he said. His voice sounded strange. I didn't like it. "She never misbehaves like this. . . ."

I wondered why Dad had stopped talking. I looked at Mom. She was staring at Ms. Davita's lap.

"Oh, no," I groaned softly.

Zoey had wet her diaper—all over Ms. Davita's lizard-print skirt!

It made my day. Maybe my whole week.

What can I say about school that day? Kids were asking me about Zoey's birthday party, which was the very next day, and I pretended to be excited. But all I could think of was that Zoey was making a really bad impression on Ms. Davita. Would she suffer for it when she reached the NO Zoo? Would Ms. Davita tell everyone Zoey was bad? Would they put her in a cage far away from all the other orangutans? Needless to say, I didn't learn anything in classes. At least it was Friday.

After school, I begged Tyler to come home with me. I needed his help in case I'd gotten some response from an e-mail pen pal. I also didn't want to run into Ms. Davita without backup. Brad had baseball practice, Dad was attending a lecture, and Mom . . . poor Mom! She'd been stuck with Ms. Davita all day at the zoo.

Anyway, Tyler was eager to check our e-mail and curious to get a glimpse of the evil Ms. Davita.

"I don't understand a zoo director who wears animal print clothes," he muttered as we climbed the stairs to Zoey's room, where I'd set up my computer. "This is more than just a case of bad taste."

Behind Tyler, I rolled my eyes. Since when had he begun to go geekoid?

We had just gotten settled at the computer when a knock on Zoey's bedroom door made me jump.

"Who is it?" I said.

The door opened, and Brad stuck his big head inside. "Hey, can I come in?"

Since when did he knock? "Okay," I said warily. "But what do you want? I thought you had practice today."

Brad came into the room and shut the door behind him. "I did. I mean, I do," he replied. "It's just that . . ."

I'd never seen my brother look so uncomfortable. It

was like he'd been caught red-handed at something incredibly embarrassing, like looking at a catalogue of women's fancy underwear.

"Just that what?" I prompted.

"I'm really going to miss Zoey, and I didn't feel like going to practice, so I came home." Brad stopped to push his glasses up on his nose. "I thought Mom and Zoey would be back by now," he added.

I didn't really know what to say. This was the second serious conversation I'd had with my brother in two days, and I was beginning to feel dizzy.

Tyler came to the rescue. "They're not home yet," he said. "We could use your help, though. Three heads are definitely better than two."

"Cool." Brad threw his baseball cap across the room and joined us at the computer. "What's up?"

Tyler and I—mostly Tyler—filled him in on what we'd discovered about the NO Zoo and on our request for an e-mail pen pal who lived near the zoo.

"Let's see if anyone's replied," Tyler said.

Someone had. It was a girl, twelve years old. Yeah! She lived about a mile from the NO Zoo, and she loved animals. She was a member of several organizations devoted to saving endangered species. Last year, she'd led a walk-a-thon in her neighborhood to raise money for the local animal shelter. To Tyler's question, "Do you have pets?" she'd answered, "I prefer to call them companions."

Her name was Sloane.

"She sounds perfect!" I was so excited I fell off my stool again. This was getting ridiculous. I stood up and put the stool in a corner. From now on, I'd stand.

"How do we reply?" Brad asked.

Tyler spent the next few minutes getting in touch with the youth service and telling them we'd—I'd— love to become Sloane's e-mail pen pal. Half an hour later, we were ready to "talk" to her.

"Let me do the typing. I mean, the talking," I said, pushing Tyler out of the desk chair.

"Okay, okay," he muttered. "Take it easy."

"Dear Sloane," I typed. "How are you? I am fine."

"That's my little sister," Brad said. "Our very own creative genius."

I turned around and stuck my tongue out at him. It wasn't as ugly as Zoey's, but it was a close second. "I'm being friendly," I explained. I continued to type. "I'm here with my brother, Brad, and my best friend, Tyler. We all love animals. In fact, we love one animal so much that we need to ask you to help us save her."

I sent that part of the message, and we waited for Sloane's reply. Luckily, she was at her computer, so it came in a few minutes.

"What's going on?" she wrote. I read her note aloud. "Oh, by the way, I'm fine. How are you? What kind of animal is in trouble? How can *I* help?"

Tyler, Brad and I spent the next hour talking with our new friend. She knew the NO Zoo really well. She went there all the time and told us about the less-than-perfect conditions she'd spotted. She also told us she'd made friends with an eighteen-year-old guy who was saving for college and then veterinary school. He had worked at the zoo every summer for years and was now there full-time. She called him the Pachyderm Coordinator. In other words, he gave little kids rides on the elephants. Sloane told us he would be a good ally on the inside. I was a bit skeptical, but Tyler and Brad agreed she should talk to him about Zoey. His name was Pete.

But what really got us excited was what Sloane told us about Ms. Davita and the Assistant Director, a guy named Hugh Sweetbreads. The loyal zoo employees, people like Pete, didn't trust them at all. Some quit their jobs in protest over Ms. Davita and Mr. Sweetbreads' methods. Others were fired when they made suggestions. Others, like Pete, kept their mouths shut but their eyes open for clues to any illegal behavior. So far, no one had seen anything.

"No conclusive evidence of wrongdoing," Tyler said, stroking his chin. He sounded like a TV lawyer.

We had just said good-bye to Sloane, with the promise of an update on Ms. Davita's odd behavior around Zoey, when we heard the front door close. Brad cocked his head. "Mom, Zoey, and the Dragon Lady," he said. "Come on, let's take Zoey off Mom's hands."

I stretched. "Good idea. Ready to meet Ms. Davita?" I asked Tyler.

He nodded. "As ready as I'll ever be."

It was two o'clock on Saturday afternoon, and the party was going strong. Our house had never been so packed full of people. Everyone was happy except my family, Tyler—and Ms. Davita. It was clear she was at the party under protest. She spent most of the time sneezing and blowing her nose. I noticed the parents of some of Dad's patients looking at her warily. They pulled their kids away from her whenever she walked by.

Zoey was in her glory. After all, she was the center of attention. Personally, I wouldn't know anything about being the center of attention. (That's a joke.) Zoey wore her purple party dress. On her head was a pointed party hat. Her face was covered with cake, ice cream, and every other type of food we'd provided. All the kids from my class wanted their picture taken with her. Mean Freddie Finkle kept everyone in line. At one point, I heard him shout, "One at a time, you bozos!" as he herded people into order.

It took a lot of energy to pretend to be happy. I even smiled at the good-natured ribbing I got from my friends about my Pin-the-Tail-on-the-Human poster. I was so mature I could have screamed.

At about three o'clock, Brad and Tyler agreed to keep an eye on Zoey while I zoomed in on Ms. Davita to see if I could get her to reveal any information—*incriminating* information, Tyler reminded me—about the NO Zoo.

For the party, Ms. Davita had chosen a fetching ensemble (I read that phrase in a fashion magazine once) of cowhide. Not only was her suit made of cowhide, but it was also black and white like a cow. I think that part was fake, but I can't be sure.

I found her sticking her head out the kitchen window and breathing deeply. Her nose was very red.

"Ms. Davita?" I asked.

I startled her. She pulled her head back inside and, in the process, crashed it into the half-open window.

I winced. "Are you hurt? Can I get you anything?"

Ms. Davita fixed me with her allergy-swollen eyes and said, "Some peace and quiet, perhaps."

"Allergies still bothering you?" I asked. A doofus could see that they were, but I had to go slow. Tyler's orders.

Clearly, Ms. Davita decided I *was* a doofus. She glared at me and didn't answer.

I changed the subject. "Ms. Davita, we love Zoey very much," I said, trying to look as earnest and as pitiful as I do when I want to stay home "sick" from school. "We're going to miss her. So we'll be coming to see her a lot. Maybe every other week."

Something about what I said frightened her, I think. Her face got a little paler, and she clutched her soggy wad of tissues even tighter. Ick.

"That's not really a good idea," she said. I think she was trying to sound sympathetic. Adults talk this way when they're trying to lie to you or give you bad news or make you stop asking questions. It's stupid. Don't they know kids see through fake stuff?

"Why not?" I asked.

Ms. Davita sighed. "Well, Zoey will have to adjust to her new environment, and the sooner she does that, the better. She shouldn't be distracted by visitors. We don't want the other orangutans resenting her because she thinks she's special, now do we?"

"But she *is* special," I said.

Ms. Davita nodded. "Well, of course she is. All creatures are special. But Zoey will have to learn how to live like her orangutan brothers and sisters."

I narrowed my eyes and took a chance. "You mean, in a dirty cage? With no place to go when she wants to get away from the people staring at her? And stale water and food that's not really fresh?"

I'd just recited some of the complaints I'd read about the NO Zoo. I watched for the impact of my words.

Ms. Davita's eyes glittered. Suddenly, I felt really scared. For a moment, she didn't say anything. When she finally spoke, I was practically soaked with cold sweat.

"Animals are not humans, my dear," she said.

"No," another voice broke in, "but I think we'd all agree they deserve respect and proper treatment."

It was my mom to the rescue. I was never so happy to see her!

Ms. Davita shifted her eyes to Mom, and her face got that bland professional look on it again. "Of course, Dr. Miles. If you'll excuse me?"

As she left the kitchen, I threw my arms around my mom and squeezed. I hadn't learned anything definitely incriminating from my conversation with Ms. Davita, but I'd gotten a pretty strong feeling she was covering up something.

"Mom, you're the best," I said. I looked up at her. "I mean it. And I'm so, so sorry about saying that you didn't care for Zoey. I didn't mean it, honest."

Mom smoothed my hair—not an easy thing to do!—

and smiled. "I know you didn't, Molly. Sometimes, when we feel angry and helpless, we lash out at the people we need the most."

I shook my head. "Weird, huh?"

"Totally," Mom agreed. "Now, I have a favor to ask you. It involves Zoey."

I pulled away and went to the refrigerator to get some soda. "Sure, Mom," I said. "Anything."

"Will you come with me and Zoey to the Northern Ohio Zoo tomorrow?" she said.

Before I could say yes, Tyler skidded into the kitchen. "Uh, Mrs. Miles, you'd better come into the living room," he said.

"What's wrong, Tyler?" Mom asked.

"I think Zoey's about to start a food fight!"

"Not again." Mom shook her head. "Come on, Molly. Let's see if we can stop it."

Tyler led the way. I followed Mom from the kitchen, a huge grin on my face. No way we were going to stop Zoey from starting a food fight if she wanted to—I only hoped it would be a good one. Just in case, I grabbed a camera from the counter on the way out.

When I reached the living room, I stopped short. In fact, I crashed into Mom, who crashed into Tyler.

Zoey was sitting on top of the armoire my mother had bought at a flea market for ten dollars and restored for about a zillion dollars. Her pointy hat was perched on the side of her head. Her brand-new purple party dress was covered with something sticky.

Mom hadn't cut Zoey's birthday cake yet, but Zoey

had. In each fist she clutched a wad of cake. Icing oozed from between her long black fingers.

"Uh, Ms. Davita?"

It was Brad. He stood to the side of the armoire, trying to keep one eye on Zoey and one on the zoo director.

"I wouldn't stand there if I were you," he warned her.

Ms. Davita stood in front of the armoire, directly in Zoey's line of fire.

"Nonsense," Ms. Davita said. "I will simply tell this . . . I will tell Zoey to come down from there at once. She might as well start learning some discipline if she is to live at *my* zoo."

"Uh, Ms. Davita . . ." my mom interjected.

Ms. Davita cut Mom off.

"Dr. Miles," she said, turning to face Mom, "I have been in this business a long time, and I assure you, a firm hand is all that is needed in situations like these."

She turned back to look up at Zoey. I cringed.

Splat!

Splat, again!

Zoey grinned and swung down from the armoire. Brad reached for her and missed. Tyler tried next and fell flat on his face. Dad came out of nowhere and slid on a wad of icing. Wuumpf!

"Food fight!" Freddie Finkle yelled as he threw a fistful of ice cream at Margie Lussman.

I looked back to Ms. Davita. She stood completely still. M & Ms whizzed by her head like minibullets. Two large splatters of wet birthday cake decorated her face, one on each cheek. A full can of shaken soda erupted over her head. I watched as the foam trickled down her neck and shoulders and made brown streaks over her cowhide ensemble. It didn't look so fetching anymore.

I couldn't help it. I raised the camera I'd taken from the kitchen and snapped.

Ms. Davita, I thought, didn't anyone ever tell you that when you live with an orangutan, it's best to wear machine-washable clothing?

I helped Mom get Zoey ready for bed that night. Her last night in our home. Did she know what was happening? I wasn't sure. I *was* sure she didn't like Ms. Davita. No one in my family did.

I spent a long time giving Zoey her bath—the food fight had been pretty bad—and helping Mom comb out the tangles in her long, red hair. What Mom didn't know was that I was secretly stashing the hair that came out on the comb. By the time we tucked Zoey into her crib, I had a big handful of hair.

Mom went off to pack for both of us and left me to watch Zoey until she fell asleep. The plan was this. Ms. Davita was flying back to the NO Zoo on one plane. Mom, Zoey, and I were going on another. Ms. Davita wanted it that way.

Dad had called an old college friend who was president at a big airline and explained our situation. We didn't want Zoey traveling in a cage in the cargo hold. Dad's friend said Zoey could travel in the passenger section of the plane as long as two of us went with her. And as long as we traveled first class.

Mom tried, but she couldn't get either the Los Angeles Zoo or the Northern Ohio Zoo to pay for the tickets. Expensivo!

I looked down at Zoey and realized she'd fallen asleep clutching my hand. After about fifteen minutes, my hand and arm were seriously numb, but I didn't have the heart to pull away. This might be the very last night I'd spend as Zoey's big sister.

I looked at the overnight bag filled with Zoey's favorite toys. The Raggedy Ann doll she slept with when she was sick. The purple dinosaur whose head she'd torn off. Mom had stitched the neck so the stuffing didn't fall out, and Zoey now chewed on it like a dog chews on a bone.

Finally, Zoey relaxed her grip on my hand, and I eased it away. As pins and needles attacked my arm, I leaned over and kissed Zoey's forehead. Then I picked up my orangutan hair stash and snuck out of Zoey's room.

At the top of the stairs I paused to listen. Good. Mom and Dad were talking to Ms. Davita. Probably making last-minute arrangements.

I hurried into my room and, without turning on a light, slipped Zoey's hair into Ms. Davita's pillowcase. I spread it out evenly so she wouldn't feel any lumps. Then I hurried back to Zoey's room.

Allergies to dust and pollen? Yeah, right. Ms. Davita was allergic to Zoey, and I was going to prove it.

It was late, and I had to get up early. I knew I should be asleep, but I wasn't.

I sat at my computer, sending e-mail to Sloane and

answering her messages. After all, if I was going to trust this person with helping me save Zoey from a miserable life at the NO Zoo, I wanted to know something more about her. After being dumped by my former friend Cyndie Barnes, I have to admit I was a bit nervous about becoming friends with another girl.

Would Sloane like me? Would I like her? Would she call me names like Brad did? Or was it only boys who called girls names? I didn't know anymore.

I wondered if we'd become good enough friends so that I'd be able to tell her about some of the goopy stuff that happened—only sometimes—when I looked at Tyler.

"Do you have brothers and sisters?" I typed. "What are they like?"

I waited for Sloane's reply.

"No," I read, when it came. "I'm an only child. I think that's why I like animals so much. Do you like having a brother? Do you ever wish you had a sister?"

I had to think about that one. Finally, I typed, "I guess I do like having a brother. Sometimes Brad is a major pain in the you-know-where. But a lot of times it's fun having him around. I play dirty tricks on him, and he did teach me to wrestle."

I hesitated before answering Sloane's next question. Did I ever want a sister? Well, I did have Zoey. I snuck a peek at my baby sister, asleep in her crib across the room. But I'm pretty sure Sloane meant did I ever wish I had a human sister.

"I don't know if I want a sister—besides Zoey," I

typed. "I don't know what having one would be like. Do you ever want one?"

After a few minutes, Sloane answered.

"I don't know, either," I read. "But I think it would be cool to have a new girlfriend. Don't you?"

I grinned and typed.

"Definitely."

I hesitated and then thought, why not?

"Do you like Clint Eastwood movies?" I typed.

Sloane's answer came.

"Definitely."

Chapter

6

"**I**s there anything I can get you?" the flight attendant asked. Her smile was big, but it looked a little plastic. I couldn't blame her. Imagine having to be nice to total strangers all day long. And imagine if one of those strangers was a year-old orangutan.

"Nope," I said. "I'm okay. But Zoey needs another barf bag." I nodded at my baby sister, who was wearing denim overalls. She sat next to me, while Mom sat just across the aisle. "She's already used the first one."

Zoey grinned and shook her head. The barf bag slid down over one eye.

The flight attendant hurried off. I shrugged.

Mom reached across the aisle and squeezed my hand. "Okay?" she asked.

"Sure, Mom," I replied. Even though the reason for our trip was totally depressing, I was enjoying traveling in first class. I'd never done it before. About every five minutes we were offered something to eat or drink, the seats were super comfortable, and I could choose from about a million different magazines.

The flight wasn't long, but I'd been up late, talking to Sloane. Then up early that morning doing last-minute packing and saying horrible good-byes. I was tired, so I decided to rest my eyes for a while. That's what my dad says when he doesn't want to admit he fell asleep in his favorite chair. He says he was just "resting his eyes."

I replayed the morning in my head and, in spite of being drowsy, began to chuckle. My scheme to prove that Ms. Davita was allergic to Zoey had worked.

At about six o'clock, I'd passed my bedroom on the way to the bathroom and heard loud wheezing coming from inside. I stopped and leaned closer to the door. Then I heard a sneezing streak you wouldn't believe. Ten sneezes in a row! I did *not* want to know how my walls looked after that.

Later, when we sat down for breakfast, Ms. Davita felt so sick she could drink only water. Her eyes were so puffy they were almost swollen shut, and her nostrils flared like butterfly wings. Would you believe I actually felt sorry for her? Not! Especially after she gave Zoey a nasty look.

The next thing I knew, someone was shaking me. "Molly, wake up!"

"What?" I straightened and stretched and yawned. "Oh, hi, Mom," I said.

Mom didn't return my greeting. "Where's Zoey?" she said, her voice tight.

"She's right . . . She *was* right there!" I cried, staring at the now empty window seat next to me. "I had her strapped in. I must have fallen asleep. . . ."

Mom sighed. "So did I. Come on, she can't have gone far."

I stood up—almost cutting myself in two by forgetting to unfasten my seatbelt first—and followed Mom to the flight attendant's station.

"Did you see my sister?" I asked loudly.

A flight attendant I hadn't seen before smiled pleasantly at me. "Well, why don't you tell me what your sister looks like?"

"She's about two feet tall and has long arms, really short legs, and lots of long red hair all over her body."

The flight attendant wasn't smiling anymore. She was frowning. "If you told me the truth, young lady," she scolded, "I might be able to help you."

That's when Mom came to the rescue. "Ms. . . . Ms. Pearce," Mom said, reading the flight attendant's name badge. "Her sister is an orangutan. She's not Molly's *real* sister, of course, but in a way . . ."

Luckily, just then we heard the distant sound of Zoey shrieking. "There she is, Mom," I said.

"Where?" Mom looked toward the back of the plane. "I think it came from coach."

In fact, Zoey's voice had come from one of the bathrooms in coach. She'd locked herself in. Mom and I stood outside, calling support and encouragement to Zoey, while a flight attendant tried to break in to the bathroom. The people in the seats close to the bathroom were laughing and enjoying the spectacle.

"I thought I was dreaming when I saw an orangutan in denim overalls lope down the aisle," I heard one older woman say. "I guess I wasn't." At least no one was mad. No one but the flight attendants, that is.

Finally, we got the bathroom door open. Zoey rushed out and jumped into my mother's arms.

"I'm sorry for all the trouble," Mom said, holding Zoey tightly. "She's just a little excited, that's all. She's never flown before."

Before anyone could answer, Mom and I scooted back toward first class. When we were seated again and Zoey's seatbelt was securely fastened, I turned to Mom.

"Do you think Zoey locked herself in the bathroom because she knows what's going on?" I whispered.

Mom shrugged. "Zoey's pretty smart, Molly. Who knows?"

I stole a look at my baby sister, who was ripping the pages out of a particularly boring magazine and tossing them over her head. Yes, I thought. Zoey knows.

After what seemed like days, we reached the NO Zoo. Normally, I would have been excited to ride in a limo (have you ever tried to flag down a taxi while holding a squirming orangutan?), but that day, I couldn't even manage a smile. While Zoey played with the intercom, electronic windows, and TV, I stared out the window at the Ohio landscape. It seemed bleak compared to home, but maybe that's because I felt so sad.

When we arrived at the zoo, Mom took Zoey into the infirmary to meet some of the staff. I headed off to find Sloane at the Elephant House. I told Mom I'd be gone most of the afternoon, but she seemed too busy to care.

For once, it didn't bother me even a little that Mom was paying more attention to Zoey than to me.

The night before, Sloane and I also had agreed to keep in touch with Tyler and Brad via e-mail, using Sloane's laptop computer. From Los Angeles, Tyler and Brad would continue to write letters, make phone calls, and gather information, all in an effort to get Zoey back. Sloane and I would do some investigating at the NO Zoo. She'd told me she was working on a plan and that she'd fill me in when we met.

I looked at the printed map I'd picked up at the dilapidated building that served as a visitors center. The Elephant House was on the other side of the zoo. I would have to hurry.

As I jogged through the zoo, I couldn't help but notice things that really upset me. Trash was rotting on the fenced-off grassy areas, which weren't very grassy. A large branch from a dead tree hung dangerously over the public walkway. I trotted past the brown bears and then trotted back. Yup. The realistic "cave" built to allow the bears some private space, away from the crowds, was boarded up! Worse, someone had spray-painted graffiti on the rough wooden boards. A little farther on, I passed the seal pool. The water looked grungy, not clean and clear and aqua blue like it was supposed to look. What was going on here?

I slowed to a walk as I approached the Elephant House. I spotted a girl standing alone. She fit the description Sloane had given me of herself. Tall. Slim. Long blonde hair in two braids. Granny glasses. Chunky sandals. Ripped jeans and a tie-dyed T-shirt. Over that, a lightweight anorak, bright purple. I'd already figured from our e-mail that I liked her. Now I knew it.

"Molly?" the girl asked.

"Sloane?"

We smiled, and as I said, "Cool anorak," she said, "Cool sneakers." They were purple. We were instant friends.

"Is Zoey here?" Sloane asked, her expression turning very serious.

"She's with my mom. They're at the infirmary," I told her. "They're going to introduce Zoey to her cousin in a little while. His name is Charlie."

Sloane nodded. "I've seen him," she said. "He doesn't look very happy. He's kind of messy and lethargic."

Now, I'm as smart as the next twelve-year-old kid, but I didn't know what "lethargic" meant. I wanted to know, but I was too embarrassed to ask.

"Lethargic, huh?" I said, squinting intelligently. "Hmmm."

Sloane shrugged. "Yeah, you know, he has no energy. He's like a couch potato."

I knew what *that* meant, all right. I'd been called one of those for years.

"Let's check out some sights," I suggested, "and then we'll meet my mom and Zoey. Remember, though, if she asks how me met, say we just bumped into each other here and started to talk. Okay?"

"Right," Sloane agreed. "We don't want anyone to know our plan."

Again with the plan! She and Tyler would get along great. "What plan?" I asked.

"Our plan to catch Ms. Davita and Mr. Sweetbreads red-handed," she explained triumphantly. "Doing something illegal."

"And just how do we do that?" I asked.

Sloane smiled and pointed to her backpack. It was pretty big. "Easy. We sneak into the zoo offices tonight and use my camcorder to catch them in the act."

"Oh, okay . . . We *what?!*"

My heart started to beat faster. Sneak in? At night? With a camcorder?

Sloane looked perfectly calm. Was my new friend a lunatic? A criminal? Or just really smart?

"It'll be okay." She smiled. "Trust me."

I looked straight at her and tried to find any trace of dishonesty. Was she trying to trick me? Get me into trouble?

No.

"But what if Ms. Davita and Mr. Sweetbreads aren't in the offices at night?" I asked. "What then?"

"Then I break into their computer files and look for evidence of wrongdoing. I'm a pretty good hacker, you know," she admitted. "Don't spread it around."

She didn't have to worry. I wouldn't. I had no intention of spending my teenage years on probation.

"Then," she continued, "I make a copy of the files, and we give the files to the police."

I could see a lot of holes—and a lot of danger—in this scheme, but I didn't have another plan. And it did sound pretty exciting. If we were lucky and found some evidence that would either shut down the zoo or get Ms. Davita fired, we'd be in a better position to get Zoey back where she belonged: home, with her family.

"Okay," I agreed. "But first, I want to meet Pete."

Sloane and I spent about an hour walking around the Zoo, going into the houses and wandering through the outdoor exhibits. Everywhere we went, we saw things we didn't like, and I took notes about them. I felt important, like I was an investigative reporter trying to uncover a scandal. While I wrote, Sloane snapped photos.

We stopped by the elephant rides to meet Sloane's friend, Pete. He was a total hunk. And way too old for us. Still, I couldn't help but see the way Sloane sort of gazed at him and played with the end of one of her braids as she talked to him. When he smiled and promised to help us in any way he could, I thought Sloane would faint.

"Will you be around for Zoey's welcoming ceremony tomorrow?" I asked as I grabbed Sloane's arm. It was so she wouldn't fall over backward.

"I wouldn't miss it," he assured me. Just then, a mother and her little boy came by to ride the "efelants," so Sloane and I headed off.

I looked at Sloane and wondered if she even knew what kind of effect Pete had on her.

"He's really, uh, cool," I said.

Sloane shrugged. "Who, Pete? Yeah, he's okay."

I rolled my eyes. She had it bad. Way worse than I did about Tyler.

"Where to now?" I asked.

Sloane made one of those exaggerated frowny-concentrating expressions and said, "Let's take a look at the offices. Just to get an idea of the layout so we don't get lost tonight. It'll be dark, you know."

I still hadn't asked Sherlock Sloane how she planned on sneaking us into the zoo, let alone how I was going to get away from my mom. Maybe I should just trust her, like she said, I thought.

I smiled. "It usually is dark at night."

Sloane punched my arm. It made me think of Tyler, who had started to do this at least once, sometimes twice, a day. I was beginning to think it meant he liked me. I mean, *liked* me. You know how in the old days boys dipped girls' braids in inkwells because they *liked* them? But when a girl hits your arm, does it mean that she likes you or that she wishes you'd shut up?

Sloane and I made our way to the zoo's central offices. The smallish building was in bad need of a new paint job, and one of the front windows had been repaired with masking tape. We didn't see anyone around, so we opened the door and went inside.

"What if someone asks us why we're here?" I whispered. "This building isn't exactly on the tour." Besides, I knew we'd better get back soon. Mom never forgot about any of her kids for too long.

"Leave it to me," Sloane whispered back.

I shrugged and looked around. We were in a small, square waiting room, decorated with two ripped plastic chairs for visitors and a half-dead potted plant. There wasn't even a poster of a wild animal. Off the small room were two doors. Both were partially opened. On one door was nailed a brass plaque that read: MS. LOLITA DAVITA, DIRECTOR. On the other was a brass plaque that read: MR. HUGH SWEETBREADS, ASSISTANT DIRECTOR. This was the place, all right.

"Do you think anyone's here?" I whispered to Sloane.

"Let's find out." Sloane paused and then cleared her throat really loudly.

"Oh, that was natural," I said, rolling my eyes.

No one came running out of either office.

"I guess we're alone," I muttered. "I'll take Sweetbreads' office, you take Davita's. Let's just look real quickly at where the desks and file drawers and computers are, okay?"

"Right." Sloane tiptoed off to Ms. Davita's office, and I went to Mr. Sweetbreads' office.

No sooner had I stepped around his half-opened door than I heard the front door open. Trapped!

Did I remain cool, calm, and collected? No. Did I panic? Yes. Absolutely.

There was no good reason I could imagine for my being in this office.

So when Mr. Hugh Sweetbreads stood in the doorway two seconds later, glaring at me, I simply stared back, mouth open, heart racing. I think I managed to say, "Uh . . ."

If I had been stunned when I first saw Ms. Davita, it was nothing to what I felt now. At least I was in my own home when the zoo director appeared. Here, I was on alien turf with the alien blocking my escape.

Mr. Sweetbreads was as short as Ms. Davita was tall; as round as she was skinny. His hair was pale yellow and hung in greasy strands along the sides of his face. His skin—what I could see of it—was so pink it looked raw, as if it had been sunburned over and over again. His nose was upturned like a pig's. His eyes were lost in the fatty folds of his face. If they were any color at all, I couldn't tell what.

After what seemed like way too long a time, he said, "What are you doing in my office?" His voice was raspy, as if he had trouble breathing.

"Uh . . ." I said again. This was getting me nowhere. It certainly wasn't getting me *out,* which was where I wanted to be.

"What did you look at?" he asked now, taking a step closer to me. "Did you touch anything? Did you?"

Just then I heard the front door open and slam shut loudly. Sloane called out, "Is anyone here? I lost my map and need to know where to get another one."

Mr. Sweetbreads glared at me with his little piggy eyes, turned, and walked into the waiting room. I scurried after him and made my way directly to the front door. I ran down to the main path and waited, out of sight of the building, for Sloane to join me.

When she did, a few minutes later, I was still trembling.

"That was close," I said.

"Tell me about it," Sloane agreed. "When I saw him go into his office, I snuck out the front door really quietly and came back in a minute later."

I shuddered. "I am so glad you did," I said. "I didn't even want to think about being alone with that guy for another minute!"

We decided we'd had enough investigating for the day and agreed to take a ride on the sky safari before joining Mom and Zoey.

Ten minutes later, we climbed into a small car on the sky safari. We were the only ones on the ride. Suddenly, I got nervous and turned back to the teenage girl taking tickets and manning the controls.

"Are you sure it's okay for us to go out alone?" I called. "Shouldn't we wait for more people?"

I couldn't hear what she said, but I did see her smile just before she pushed a button that sent Sloane and me off with a lurch.

Sloane seemed to be enjoying what little scenery there was, although we both wondered why we couldn't spot any birds or animals. I, on the other hand, was a nervous wreck. Being caught by Mr. Sweetbreads had really spooked me. There was something about him, and about Ms. Davita, I just didn't trust. Something . . .

We both screamed. I am proud to say I screamed louder than Sloane did.

Our little sky safari car had stopped moving. It was hanging awkwardly from the main cable, almost on its side. Something was very, very wrong. I was afraid that if we were going anywhere, it could only be down.

"Don't breathe," Sloane whispered.

"Not a problem," I whispered back. I was happy to sit perfectly still and wait to be rescued.

But that's not what happened.

Suddenly, the car started again with a jolt.

"We're never going to make it!" I whispered frantically.

Sloane didn't say anything. I don't think she could. She looked almost as if she was in a state of shock.

The car screeched along, slowly, until it reached the end of the main cable. Then it lumbered into the loading dock, where a frantic zoo employee, another teenage girl, helped us out of the car.

"I'm so sorry! What happened? Are you all right? I've sent for a repair crew and an ambulance. . . ."

I managed to assure her that we were fine but that we were really late to meet someone and had to go. I grabbed Sloane's hand and pulled her after me. She still didn't speak as we ran down the fake, winding jungle path that led from the sky safari.

When we reached the entrance/exit to the ride, I stopped short. Sloane crashed into me, but I didn't care.

Standing there, an evil smile on his face, was Mr. Sweetbreads. I was out of breath, out of screams, and out-of-my-mind scared.

"Have a nice ride, girls?" he leered. Then, with a chuckle, he was gone.

Chapter 7

On our way to the Primate House, Sloane and I decided that even if the sky safari ride was old and rickety to begin with—and it probably was—Mr. Sweetbreads definitely had something to do with our "accident." This made us really scared but also more determined to get hard evidence against both him and Ms. Davita.

"Don't mention the sky safari thing to my mom," I warned Sloane. My heart was still beating fast, and my knees were still weak. "She'll really freak out and send me home before we can get our evidence."

I have to admit, at that moment going home didn't sound too bad. That guy Sweetbreads really gave me the creeps.

Sloane laughed, though she still held my arm in a death grip. "There are so many things I'm not supposed to tell your mother. I'm almost afraid to say hello!"

I frowned. "I'm sorry, Sloane. My family hates to keep secrets from each other, and usually I wouldn't do this kind of thing, but . . ."

Sloane shrugged. "It's no big deal. Hey, here we are."

We went inside the Primate House and asked a keeper where we could find Dr. Miles. He pointed to a door marked "Private." When I knocked, another keeper answered, and once again, I asked for my mom. When I told him I was Molly Miles, he smiled and showed us inside.

Sloane elbowed me. "You celeb, you."

I liked it, but I pretended to be cool. "Comes with the territory. Zoey!"

Mom and Zoey were sitting together on a couch. When she saw me, Zoey stuffed her headless purple dinosaur doll into a pocket of her overalls and loped over.

"Uufff!" I grunted as she leaped into my arms. "I missed you too, Zoey," I murmured, holding her tight. "Zoey, Mom, meet my new friend, Sloane."

My mother smiled. "Nice to meet you, Sloane. What do you think of our little girl?"

Sloane reached out to scratch Zoey's head. "She's adorable, Dr. Miles. Has she met Charlie yet?"

"How do you know Charlie?" Mom asked while I sat on the couch with Zoey. In the past few months, she had gotten too heavy for me to hold for long while standing.

Sloane explained that she lived nearby and was involved in a lot of animal causes. "And I have a cat and a dog," she said. "I love animals."

I spotted a shrewd twinkle in Mom's eyes, and before I could interrupt, she said, "How did you girls meet?"

At the same time I blurted, "At the seal pool," Sloane blurted, "By the zebras."

I could see Mom was holding back a smile. "I see," she said. "You do agree that you met for the first time today?"

That was easy. We both said, "Yes."

Mom shrugged. "Okay. Well, I think we should introduce Zoey to Charlie now. Come on."

The three of us, Zoey holding my left hand and Sloane's right, followed Mom out of the room and into a private space behind the animals' display area.

I was really hoping Zoey and Charlie would hit it off, like Sloane and I had. If they could be friends as well as cousins, I wouldn't feel as terrible about leaving her at the NO Zoo.

Charlie was waiting for us with a keeper named Martin.

He was the saddest thing I'd ever seen. Sloane was right. Charlie was lethargic. Not only that, he was listless. His hair was matted and his eyes were dull. He looked at Zoey and lowered his eyes.

"Mom, what's wrong with him?" I stage-whispered.

Mom shook her head. Her face was grim. "I don't know for sure, Molly. But I'd guess he's depressed."

Mom turned to the keeper, a man with a nice face. "How's Charlie's physical health?" she asked.

"Fine, Dr. Miles," Martin responded. "Except that he's a little overweight because he doesn't get much exercise. I think you're right. Charlie's depressed." Martin smiled sadly and smoothed Charlie's head. The orangutan's expression didn't change.

I looked at Mom and she nodded. "Zoey," I said,

crouching by her side, "say hello to your cousin Charlie. He's sad. Maybe you can make him happy."

Sloane crouched on Zoey's other side. "He needs a friend, Zoey," she said softly.

Zoey pulled her headless purple dinosaur from her pocket and loped over to where Charlie sat with Martin. I held my breath. She stopped about two feet in front of him and made a sad face. Charlie looked at her. Then she held out the dinosaur to him.

We waited. None of us made a sound. I glanced quickly at Mom and saw the tension in her face. Martin was biting his lip. For a moment, Charlie stared at the dinosaur.

And then he slowly reached out and took it from Zoey. She made a small sound and nodded. Charlie studied the dinosaur for another moment, and then he stuffed it in his mouth.

Zoey screeched. She walked the two feet to her cousin and threw herself in his arms. Charlie didn't hug her back at first, but then, slowly, tentatively, he put his arms around her and squeezed.

"Well, I'll be," whispered Martin. "That's the first time Charlie's ever done that," he declared. "Maybe Zoey's just what he needs!"

Mom beamed so hard I thought her face would split. Sloane and I hugged each other. Leave it to Zoey, I thought proudly.

The four of us watched as Zoey broke the hug and instantly became the bossy sister. She pushed at Charlie until he stood, and then she tried to make him dance with her. He looked a little annoyed, but once he started moving, his excitement grew.

"They remind me of you and Brad," Mom said to me.

"No way!" I protested. "Brad's uglier!"

Mom drove Sloane and me to the motel where Mom and I were staying, and then she drove the borrowed van back to the zoo. It was the first night Zoey would spend away from our home, and Mom had arranged to stay with her.

Before she headed back to the zoo, she turned to Sloane. "How are you getting home? Do you want me to drop you off on my way back to the zoo?" she asked.

Sloane shook her head. "That's okay, Dr. Miles. I'll call my parents. They know I'm with . . . I mean, they know I always call them when I need a ride. Don't worry, I won't do anything stupid, like hitchhike."

Mom gave me another one of those meaningful looks, the kind mothers give their kids when they want them to pay extra attention. "No," Mom said to Sloane, "I'm sure you won't do anything stupid *or* dangerous."

I was surprised Mom didn't push the issue, but I guess she trusted me. Looking back on it now, I'm really glad she did. I mean, I actually *did* do something stupid and dangerous but . . . Now I'm jumping ahead.

When Mom was gone, I collapsed on one of the beds. "That was close!" I said.

Sloane dropped her backpack on the other bed. "I know, I'm sorry. Let's talk to Tyler and Brad!"

Sloane began to unpack her bag. I sat up and stared.

First, a camcorder. Then the camera I'd seen her use earlier. Next, her laptop and battery power pack. A notebook. A moldy orange. A packet of nuts. A sweatshirt. A big flashlight. A penlight. It was like being at the circus and watching about twenty clowns pile out of a teeny tiny car. You think there's no way they could all fit in there!

"You've got to be kidding!" I said. "How do you carry all that stuff without falling over?"

Sloane surveyed the contents of her backpack and shrugged. "I don't know. It's not that much. Anyway, let's get started."

While Sloane set up the computer, I opened the bags of fast food Mom had bought for us on the way to the motel. There was enough to feed an army—or two twelve-year-old girls on a secret mission.

I brought some of the food over to the bed where Sloane had set up the computer and flopped down next to her.

"Thanks," she said, reaching for a paper carton of cheese fries. "I'm starved. And I'm almost ready here."

While I chewed my hamburger and waited for Sloane to connect to Tyler and Brad, I thought about Zoey and Charlie dancing around in the Primate House. She'd looked so . . . I don't know, like she belonged with Charlie. Like I belonged with Brad?

"Sloane," I said thoughtfully, "do you think Zoey would be happier living with other orangutans than with my brother and me? Maybe she *should* live at a zoo—not the NO Zoo, but a good one, close to us. Maybe . . ."

Sloane put her hand on my arm and looked at me. "No, Molly, I don't think so. At least, not until she's older."

"But she looked so happy playing with Charlie," I said quietly. "Maybe we're not doing the right thing."

"No," Sloane said. "No, Molly. Zoey needs you."

I smiled. "And I need Zoey. I was just checking to make sure I wasn't being totally selfish about wanting her back home."

"You're not." Sloane turned back to the computer. "Look," she said. "Tyler's here. And Brad."

Sloane's fingers flew over the keyboard as she told Tyler and Brad all about our day at the zoo. When she got to the part about the near-accident on the sky safari, I made sure she told the guys we were pretty sure it was no accident.

When she was finished typing, we waited for Tyler's reply. A few minutes later, it came.

"'Be careful,'" I read aloud. "'Do you know what "sweetbreads" are? People eat them. They're made of the thymus gland of a calf. The thymus gland is part of the brain.'"

I gulped and looked at Sloane. "No way. You think he's serious?"

Sloane shuddered. "Who knows? But I, personally, am never eating sweetbreads, ever."

I looked back to the screen and continued to read what Tyler had written. "'Brad wants to know if Sloane is cute. Ow. He just punched me. Anyway, today we got on a kids' chat line and started spreading the word about Zoey being taken to NO Zoo. Brad still thinks we can't do anything because we're kids, but I say we've got to try. Brad says to make sure you guys don't think he's a wimp or anything. He says he's just being practical, like his father.'"

I made a face. "Practical like Dad? Does he have another father I don't know about?"

"Spreading the word . . . That's not a bad idea. In fact, we could start right now." Sloane's face suddenly seemed to glow with excitement. Or maybe it was the greasy cheese fries. Anyway, she said, "Let's send e-mail to the local newspapers, telling our side of the story. I bet they're planning on having some reporters at Zoey's welcoming celebration, anyway. We'll give them a new angle to the story!"

Sloane's excitement was catching. "Great," I said. "And let's send e-mail to some local schools."

"And to all of the clubs I belong to," Sloane added.

We worked for about an hour, first telling Tyler and Brad what we were doing and asking them to do the same in Los Angeles. Then we sent what Sloane called "cries for help" to every local group or school we could think of that might be interested in coming to the ceremony and showing support for Zoey. I'd never done any work for a cause before, and it was exciting.

Finally, it was time for us to sneak back into the zoo and act like detectives. I was pretty scared. I thought about Ms. Davita, whom I hadn't seen all day—I wondered where she'd gone—and about Mr. Sweetbreads, and I shuddered. What a pair. I wouldn't put it past them to make sweetbreads of Sloane and me if they caught us.

Needless to say, figuring out how to get back to the zoo was problem number one. Obviously, Sloane and I didn't drive, and we had no access to a car. We didn't have any bikes, and hitchhiking was definitely out.

We ended up taking a taxi back to the zoo. It wasn't easy to get one. When we looked in the Greenfield phone book, we found only one taxi company. At first the woman on the phone didn't want to send a taxi to pick up two kids. When we finally convinced her we were serious, she said okay, but that if we were joking, she'd have to tell our parents. Sheesh. "I have a feeling I'm not in L.A. anymore," I muttered when I hung up.

We had the taxi drop us off a few blocks from the zoo, in front of some private houses. We didn't want to let the driver know where we were really going. I had a feeling they weren't cool about kids being out at night in this town, let alone kids who were planning to break into a zoo.

I wasn't cool about breaking the law, and I was pretty sure that's exactly what we were doing by sneaking into the zoo after it had closed to visitors for the night.

I got this picture of my mom standing over me screaming, "You did *what!?*" and suddenly I felt sick to my stomach. I grabbed Sloane's arm. "I can't do this," I said. "I just can't."

It was dark. I could hear wind rustling the leaves of the trees and the call of a night bird. Eerie sounds.

Sloane pulled me closer to the fence, which we had

to climb over. If anyone drove by, they'd never see us now.

"Molly, you have to go through with it," she whispered.

I shook my head and pulled my jacket tighter around me. "No, I can't. What if we get caught? How will I ever explain to my parents? I don't want to get in trouble."

Sloane sighed. "Neither do I, Molly. Believe me, if I got caught sneaking into the zoo after hours, I would be in major trouble with my family, and my father— well, he'd be in even bigger trouble. . . ."

"Why?" I asked. "What do you mean?"

"Never mind. Just remember why we're doing this. We know Ms. Davita and Mr. Sweetbreads are up to something bad. We just don't have any real evidence. If we don't do something to expose or stop them, you and your mom will get on a plane and Zoey will stay here, all by herself, and you might never see her again." Sloane paused. "Too many animals have mysteriously died at this zoo, Molly," she said, her voice grim. "We can't let it go on. Are you with me?"

I felt terrible that I'd almost chickened out and grateful to Sloane for reminding me why we were there.

I gave her a weak smile.

"I'm with you."

Chapter
8

"**O**w! That was my foot!" Sloane hopped on her left leg and held her right foot off the ground.

"Shh! Sorry. I can't see anything," I complained.

"I told you we can't use the flashlight out here. What if someone sees us from the road?" Sloane whispered.

"I know, I know. Let's just keep going." I took Sloane's hand and led the way. I have a pretty good sense of direction, and I was sure we were heading straight for the office building.

As we walked, we kept on the lookout for any movement that might mean we were being watched. We figured there had to be a security system in place, maybe cameras and definitely a guard or two. We both admitted to having forgotten to scope out the security system earlier. So much for careers as super sleuths.

We saw nothing. But we heard a million sounds. Night birds and wind. Metal rings clanging on metal poles. An occasional grumbling as we passed the animal houses.

"Shouldn't they all be asleep?" I whispered.

"Shouldn't *we?*" Sloane replied.

"You're not losing your nerve, are you?" I asked,

turning back to face her. "You were the one who talked me into this, you know."

Sloane gave me a small shove forward. "Of course not. Would someone who thinks Clint Eastwood is the coolest lose her nerve? No way. Come on."

Finally, we reached the offices.

"Now what?" I whispered.

Sloane dropped to the ground and began to dig through her backpack. "Ta-da!" She held up a small leather pouch.

"What is it?" I asked.

"My breaking-and-entering kit," she said, unzipping the pouch and standing. "Would you hold my backpack while I get us inside?"

Right then I decided that Sloane was the most resourceful person I'd ever met. And the nuttiest.

I gulped. "Uh, sure," I said, hauling the thousand-pound bag onto my shoulder. No wonder Sloane was so thin. Carrying this around was a major workout.

"I also need you to hold the flashlight directly on the lock," Sloane instructed, handing me the penlight. "Don't flash it around."

"Don't worry," I promised. I shone the narrow beam of light onto the lock while Sloane got to work. She was amazing. In less than a minute, the lock clicked open and we slipped inside.

"Where'd you learn to do that?" I whispered.

Sloane smiled mischievously. "I've been around."

I snorted and lowered the backpack to the floor. Sloane took out a packet of computer disks.

"First, the computers," Sloane whispered.

I followed her into Ms. Davita's office and closed the door. There wasn't much for me to do except keep an eye out for anyone coming toward the building. I tiptoed from the small, grimy window to the door of Ms. Davita's office, listening and watching while Sloane worked.

And muttered. Sitting at the desk, with only the light from the computer screen and her penlight, staring intently at the screen and muttering, Sloane reminded me of a mad, brilliant scientist.

It seemed to take forever. At one point, I thought I saw a light flash in the wooded area behind the building. My stomach fell about a hundred miles.

"Hurry up," I hissed.

"Bingo!" she whispered. "Molly, check this out."

I left my post at the window and hurried over to where Sloane sat at Ms. Davita's desk.

"Look," Sloane said, pointing to the screen. "This is a letter of agreement between Ms. Davita—not the zoo, officially—and something called Uncle Bob's Traveling Animal Show. Last April, Ms. Davita sold a snow leopard cub to them for . . . Wow! That's a lot of money!"

I stared at the line of zeroes and whistled. "The white tiger is an endangered species. I can't believe this is going on right under everybody's noses!"

Sloane tapped her chin. "Last April . . . That's it!"

"What's what?" I asked.

"Last April," Sloane began excitedly, "the local papers reported that a snow leopard cub here at the zoo had died. But don't you see, Molly? The cub didn't die.

It was sold to Uncle Bob's Traveling Animal Show!"

I started to tremble. This was horrible—and wonderful. If we could track down all the animals who were supposed to have died at the NO Zoo, we'd be able to bring them home to good zoos, where they'd be well taken care of. Who knew how this Uncle Bob guy treated his animals? Anyone who would secretly buy endangered species from a zoo had to be mean and awful.

Sloane was typing away. A moment later, she said, "Here's another letter, to another traveling animal show. This time, Ms. Davita sold a hooded crane and Mr. Sweetbreads delivered it personally."

Suddenly, I felt a prickle of fear and stood perfectly still. Had I heard something out on the path? That light I'd seen flash . . . I put my hand on Sloane's arm, and when she looked up, I held my finger to my lips. I listened. After a moment, I decided I'd imagined the noise.

"Hurry," I whispered. "I don't know how much more of this I can take. See if you can find anything about Zoey and then copy the file."

Sloane nodded. The more I learned about Ms. Davita and Mr. Sweetbreads, the more frightened I got. Now I *really* didn't want to run into them.

Too late. Just as Sloane was about to start typing again, I heard the front door open.

Sloane and I looked at each other. Her face wore an expression of panic. I know mine did. We were trapped!

"The papers are in my office." That raspy voice could only belong to Mr. Sweetbreads. "We can get the other files from your office later."

We listened as two pairs of footsteps walked toward and then entered Mr. Sweetbreads' office. When the footsteps stopped, I motioned to Sloane to follow me. I looked at the small grimy window and hoped we could fit through.

I gingerly picked up the folding chair that served as the guest chair and placed it just under the window. Meanwhile, Sloane was silently stuffing everything she'd taken out of her backpack into it again.

I watched in fascinated horror as a pencil slowly rolled toward the edge of the desk. I was too afraid to say anything or to move.

It bounced onto the floor. It was the loudest pencil I'd ever heard.

"What was that? Did you hear anything?" Ms. Davita's voice sliced through the silence.

Sloane and I froze, our eyes locked onto each other's.

"Probably just one of those stupid birds," Mr. Sweetbreads answered.

I breathed for what seemed like the first time in hours and nodded toward the window.

Sloane went first. When she stepped on the chair it screeched. I almost died. Hurry, I prayed silently. She made it through the window easily. I handed her the backpack, and together, with Sloane pulling and me pushing, we got it through. I followed.

Just in the nick of time, too. As Sloane and I flattened ourselves against the building's outer wall, we heard Ms. Davita and Mr. Sweetbreads enter her office.

Would they notice the chair by the wall? Had Sloane left the computer exactly the same way she'd found it? What about the pencil on the floor?

I heard their voices as they moved around the office, but my heart was pounding so loudly, I couldn't actually hear what they said.

I looked at Sloane. She'd taken the camcorder out of the backpack and motioned for me to stay where I was.

"What?" I mouthed. "Are you crazy?"

Sloane shrugged, and very, very quietly, she began to sneak around the side of the building. I followed, scooping up the backpack along the way.

When we reached the front of the building, I saw that the door had been left ajar.

I pulled Sloane close to me. "Are you insane?" I mouthed directly into her ear.

Sloane moved away and pointed to a clump of bushes off to the side. I shook my head and, after putting the backpack against the wall, followed her into the building. What else could I do? Let her go in there alone with two creepozoids?

We quickly ducked behind the sickly potted plant. It was poor cover, but it was all we had.

I saw Sloane aim the camcorder at the half-open office door and hit the power switch.

From where we crouched, we had a partial view of both Ms. Davita and Mr. Sweetbreads. And we could hear everything.

"Have you drawn up the agreement of purchase?" Ms. Davita asked, shuffling through some files on her desk.

"Of course, my dear," her companion answered. "A representative of Wacky Wendy's Animal World will pick up that obnoxious little orangutan exactly one week from tonight."

I bit down so hard on my lip to prevent myself from screaming, I almost screamed. Ms. Davita and Mr. Sweetbreads were incriminating themselves, and they had no idea they were doing it!

"And what story will we give the press this time?" Ms. Davita cackled. "An undetected allergy to a common medication? A sudden heart attack, brought on by the trauma of leaving that ridiculous family, the Mileses?"

Good thing I'm supposed to be hiding, I thought. Nobody makes fun of my family but me! I wanted to punch Ms. Davita in her snotty nose.

Mr. Sweetbreads huffed and puffed. I think he was trying to laugh. "No, darling," he said. "Actually, I was thinking it might be fun to kill two birds with one stone—as it were. I'm going to arrange a rumor of a little fight between Zoey and Charlie. Zoey, unfortunately, being so much smaller, will be killed. Charlie, having finally lost his temper after so many months of severe depression, will have to be put down. To insure the safety of the other orangutans, of course."

Ms. Davita cackled again, louder this time. "Brilliant, darling! Zoey will be off to her new life as a performer, and Charlie will no longer be a burden on us. But now we must finish here and leave."

Sloane and I didn't wait to hear any more. We crept out of the room as quietly as we'd crept in. Once outside, I grabbed the backpack, and together we ran for the main path. Soon we found ourselves back at the section of fence we'd climbed over earlier.

Another five minutes brought us to an all-night diner. I called the taxi company to send a cab and then joined Sloane at a table in the back. She had ordered two ice cream sodas, chocolate for me and blueberry for her.

"Whew," I said, collapsing onto the bench across from Sloane. "Convincing that old bat to send a taxi was almost harder than sneaking into the zoo and getting out without being caught. They've only got one car out tonight, and someone had to go to the airport. I . . ."

Sloane's face was a sickly shade of white. Tears brimmed in her eyes.

"What's wrong!" I cried. "Are you okay?"

The tears that had been brimming now spilled down her cheeks.

"Sloane," I said, reaching for her hand, "what is it? Are you sick?"

Slowly, Sloane shook her head. Then she sighed the sorriest sigh I ever heard.

"Molly, I'm so sorry," she said. "Please forgive me."

I smiled to reassure her that no matter what had happened, we'd still be friends.

"It can't be that bad," I said, squeezing her hand. "Come on, tell me."

Sloane took a deep breath and looked me in the eye.

"I forgot to put a tape in the camcorder. We have no proof of anything, Molly. We have nothing."

Chapter 9

"**A**re you sure you're okay, Molly? You look a little tired." Mom put her wrist to my forehead and frowned. "Well," she said, "you don't have a fever."

I resisted the urge to wiggle away. "Really, Mom, I'm fine," I said. "It's just that I didn't get much sleep last night. I . . . I was thinking of Zoey."

Mom smiled and hugged me. "I know, honey. But for Zoey's sake, we have to be brave. We can't let her see how sad we are, okay?"

I smiled. I was brave. So brave I'd snuck into the zoo, the zoo's office, and the zoo's computer files. And for what? Sloane and I hadn't had time to copy any of the files. And we'd forgotten to put a tape in the camcorder.

Did you notice I said *"we'd* forgotten"? I couldn't let Sloane take the blame. After all, Zoey was *my* sister, and Sloane had done all these fabulous things to help me save her. It was her idea to do the e-mail mailing and her knowledge of computers that got us into the zoo's system in the first place. I at least could have checked the camcorder for a tape.

Mom looked at her watch. "I've got to meet the curator of the Mammal Department now. Molly, try to have a good time. I'll see you at the grandstand at noon, okay?"

"Okay, Mom." I hugged her and watched as she walked away from the Primate House. Talk about brave, I thought. Mom was incredible. Her youngest daughter was being officially adopted today, and all she was concerned about was making sure Zoey was happy.

"Hey."

I turned and squinted. The sun was bright, even though it was only ten o'clock in the morning. It was going to be a beautiful day.

"Hey, yourself," I said to Sloane. As planned, we were meeting on the steps of the Primate House.

Sloane looked as tense as I felt. The taxi had dropped me back at the motel about fifteen minutes before Mom came in from spending the night with Zoey. I'd thrown myself under the covers and pretended to be asleep. Nothing like sweating under the covers in the same clothes you've worn all day and night.

Also as planned, Sloane had brought the empty video tape and a blank diskette with her. *We* knew they were blank. But no one else did. We were going to confront Ms. Davita and Mr. Sweetbreads with what we knew. We were going to threaten to give the cassette and diskette to the police if they didn't confess and arrange to have Zoey transferred back to us *and* quit their jobs.

Maybe it would work. Maybe it wouldn't. But after everything we'd been through—running into Mr. Sweetbreads in his office, the near miss on the sky safari, and the close calls the night before—we just couldn't give up now.

Anyway, I was kind of proud of the idea. Bluffing is one of my strengths.

"Ready?" Sloane asked. She might have looked tense, but she also looked really cool. She was wearing a pink jean jacket with a painting of a panda on the back. (She whirled to show me.)

"As I'll ever be," I replied. "Nice jacket."

"Thanks. Nice T-shirt."

I smiled. It was a picture Zoey had painted. It was so good I'd had it reproduced on a T-shirt.

"Thanks," I said. "Zoey did it. It's me!"

Sloane gave me a look that made me squirm.

"What?" I said.

"Nothing, except . . . Are you sure you don't want to spend the morning with Zoey? If our plan doesn't work, this is the last day you have to spend with her."

"No!" I shouted. I hadn't meant to.

"Okay," Sloane said quietly.

"I'm sorry, Sloane," I said. "I didn't mean to yell. It's just that . . ."

How could I explain that I was afraid seeing Zoey— what I wanted most to do—would be just too painful?

Sloane reached out and hugged me.

"You don't have to explain," she said. "I understand. I'm your friend."

I smiled a really big smile. "Yeah," I said. "I know. And I'm your friend. Isn't it cool?"

Sloane wouldn't replace Tyler. But that was okay; she didn't have to. She could be my other best friend.

Together we began to walk toward some of the small

booths that had been set up by the zoo staff. Ms. Davita and Mr. Sweetbreads didn't want to spend much on the celebration, even though bringing people from the community into the zoo and getting them involved was supposed to be a priority. Tyler and I had learned that on our Internet search.

The staff made up for the lack of money with lots of creative genius. Some had made food at home and brought it to the zoo to sell. Sloane and I had a hard time getting away from the cookie and brownie stand. Together, we must have supported the feeding of three elephants for a week. Others had made costumes to wear, like the woman from the Lion House who came dressed as a Bengal tiger.

"That's what I'm going as next Halloween," I told Sloane.

"Hey, girls!"

It was Martin, the keeper who took care of Charlie. Sloane and I joined him at the Primate Booth.

"Hi, Martin," I said. "How's Charlie?"

Martin smiled. "I can't tell you girls what a difference Zoey has made. Charlie finally seems to be coming out of his depression. He's such a good guy," Martin said. "I've been so worried about him."

My heart sank when I saw the tears of happiness in Martin's eyes. He really loved Charlie. What would happen to Martin if Ms. Davita and Mr. Sweetbreads succeeded in their diabolical scheme?

For Martin's sake, as well as for Charlie's and Zoey's and everybody else's, we *had* to stop them!

"Martin," Sloane asked, pointing to a booth, "is that?"

Martin turned to look and shook his head. "It's not my idea, I can tell you that. That's Mr. Sweetbreads' design," he said. He sounded disgusted.

Sloane was pointing to a bright orange T-shirt. Across the front was printed ORANGUTANS R US!

"He thinks these cheap souvenirs will bring in money for the zoo," Martin explained.

I'm no marketing person, but I had a feeling the T-shirt *I'd* made said a lot more about orangutans than that ugly orange thing. I shuddered.

Sloane and I talked to Martin for a few minutes and then went on to see the other booths.

As the morning passed, the zoo grew more crowded. We waded through a throng of families, all smiling and laughing and enjoying themselves with the games and food and animals. It was easy to forget why we were there. Almost. Only Sloane and I knew that behind the fun lurked the two most evil people we'd ever met.

We found Pete by a special ring that had been set up in the middle of a small field. He was giving elephant rides to children and teaching them about elephants. When we came by, he was showing a group of kids the parts of an elephant's foot.

Sloane looked like she was going to fall into staring mode, so I just waved and pulled her after me. It was almost time to head to the grandstand, the place where Zoey's official handing-over and welcome were to take place. The place where we would confront Ms. Davita and Mr. Sweetbreads.

"Are you nervous?" I asked Sloane.

She nodded. "Totally."

Suddenly, I was aware of all the junk food I'd just eaten. It seemed like every greasy, sticky, gooey bite of it had formed a big greasy, sticky, gooey ball that was trying to bounce out of my mouth.

We didn't say anything else as we walked toward the grandstand, which had been set up behind the Primate House. A crowd had already gathered. Reporters from all the local papers and television stations were there, with their microphones and note pads and cameras. Had they read our e-mail? Did they know what was really happening? Would one of them ask a question about the poor conditions at the zoo? Would any of our efforts pay off?

I looked around. I didn't see Mom. She was probably with Zoey, getting her ready for her big moment.

Suddenly, I sensed a movement in the crowd in front of us and realized the ceremony was about to begin. Now was our chance.

"Come on," I said, yanking Sloane after me. "It's now or never."

Together we pushed through the crowd to the front of the grandstand. I spotted Ms. Davita and Mr. Sweetbreads, standing off to the side, heads together. What are they plotting now? I wondered. Sloane and I slipped closer.

"Just keep that monkey away from me," Ms. Davita hissed. "If I get within five feet of it I sneeze."

Mr. Sweetbreads laughed. "Don't worry, my dear. I'll take care of it. Besides, that annoyingly earnest Mrs. Miles will be with her."

"And I'll be with her, too," I said loudly. My fists were clenched. I could barely control myself.

"So will I." It was Sloane.

Ms. Davita sneered.

"Well," she said, "what have we here? Are you still hoping to get your stupid little monkey back?"

"She's not a monkey," I replied, my voice cold. "And if you were who you pretend to be, you'd know that. But you're nothing but a liar and an animal abuser. You, too, Mr. Sweetbreads," I added, turning to look at Ms. Davita's partner in crime.

Mr. Sweetbreads snorted. "We don't have time for this nonsense," he said. "If you'll excuse us . . ."

"Oh, I think you have time for these," I said, waving the video cassette and computer diskette.

Ms. Davita put her hand to her throat. "What . . . what are those?" she said, her voice tight.

"Only proof that you two are involved in the illegal selling of endangered species to traveling animal shows," Sloane said. "Does 'Uncle Bob's' ring a bell?"

"We know everything," I added. "And we want to make a deal."

Again, Mr. Sweetbreads snorted. "Ridiculous." He fixed me with his piggy eyes. "I don't believe you have any evidence of anything."

"Do you feel lucky?" I asked. I swear, I'd waited all my life to say that line! Clint would have been so proud!

There was a moment of silence. I could see Ms. Davita and Mr. Sweetbreads weighing their options and Sloane, momentarily, fighting a laugh. Finally, Ms. Davita spoke.

"What kind of deal?" she asked, her voice unsteady.

"We want . . ."

Before I could go any further, I was interrupted by a swelling of voices. The crowd around us murmured and turned, as if it were one big body. The voices, chanting now, came closer.

"What's going on?" Sloane said.

"I don't know," I answered.

But then I saw and my mouth fell open. About a hundred kids carrying signs and banners were surging toward the grandstand. They were chanting something, but I couldn't make out what.

And then everything exploded.

Out of the corner of my eye, I saw movement. Ms. Davita was reaching for the video cassette and diskette, and I was falling in an effort not to let them go.

Just as I hit the ground with an "Oof" and Ms. Davita loomed over me, a hairy red hand grabbed the cassette and diskette from my fingers.

"Zoey!" I cried. "Zoey, it's hide-and-seek! I'm it, Zoey. Hide, hide!"

Zoey screeched and loped off. I saw her take hold of the bunting on the grandstand and swing up. Then she was gone. With Zoey's talent for hiding, no one would find her for hours. We were safe!

"Stop that ape!" Ms. Davita screamed.

I scrambled to my feet just as a reporter and a cameraman rushed over. Mr. Sweetbreads didn't see them. He was staring after Zoey.

"When I get my hands on that orangutan, I'll strangle her," he cried, shaking his fist in the air.

"Interesting," the reporter said. "Mr. Sweetbreads, can you comment on the rumors of neglect at the Northern Ohio Zoo?"

"Ms. Davita," another reporter shouted, "can you explain why you were trying to attack this young girl?"

I couldn't believe what was happening. It was too good to be true. I had to find Mom. She was either going to kill me for telling Zoey to hide or hug me to death for exposing Ms. Davita and Mr. Sweetbreads as fakes. I was dying to know which. While reporters and cameramen swarmed over Ms. Davita and Mr. Sweetbreads, I grabbed Sloane's hand and ran toward the crowd of kids.

Now I could hear what they were chanting. "SEND ZOEY HOME!"

"Where did they come from?" Sloane panted as the group gathered at the foot of the grandstand.

I shook my head. "I don't know, but it must have something to do with those e-mail messages we sent yesterday."

"I can't believe it!" Sloane laughed. "See, Tyler was right and Brad was wrong. Kids *do* have power!"

"I never doubted it for a minute!" I grinned.

A tall, slim man made his way through the group of chanting kids. He was wearing a "Save the Whales" T-shirt and a pair of jeans. He looked just like . . .

"Dad!" Sloane darted off to greet her father. He grabbed her in a one-armed hug as he continued toward the grandstand. When he reached the steps, he whispered something to Sloane. I saw her smile, and then she ran toward me.

"Dad says we should join him on the grandstand," Sloane said, taking my hand. "Come on!"

I trotted along with Sloane. "I didn't know you told your dad about Zoey," I said. "Is he a vet or something?"

Sloane stopped on the stair above me and turned back. Her grin was huge.

"I didn't tell him. And no, he's not a vet. He's our mayor."

"What!" I cried. "Why didn't you tell me?"

Sloane laughed. "You never asked. Come on!"

We reached the stage. Mom was there, holding Zoey, who was clutching the blank video cassette and computer diskette in one hand. Martin was there, too. He held Charlie's hand. Charlie hooted when he saw us and took a big bite out of Zoey's purple dinosaur.

I ran over to Mom and Zoey and hugged them both as they were hugging me.

"How'd you find Zoey, Mom?" I asked. "I can never find her when she hides."

Mom smiled smugly. "Well, I *am* her mother, you know, and mothers know everything."

I rolled my eyes and hugged her again.

Just then, Sloane's dad tapped the microphone and cleared his throat. Sloane stood behind him, beaming.

"Hello, everyone," he cried.

A roaring cheer rose from the mob of kids and families. Photographers snapped pictures of the scene.

"As most of you know, I'm Mayor Powers . . ."

Another huge cheer drowned out the mayor. He raised his hands for quiet.

"Thank you," he said. "But I'm not the one you should be applauding. Some of you here today may not be aware that Greenfield has been watching some of the practices at the zoo very closely. Recently, we joined forces with a special task force appointed by the American Zoo and Aquarium Association to help uncover illegal practices and to institute a program to radically improve conditions.

"Today," he continued, "is the first day of a new life for Northern Ohio Zoo. The current director and assistant director will no longer hold those positions. In fact," he added, gesturing off to the right, where I could see Ms. Davita and Mr. Sweetbreads being led away in handcuffs, "they have accepted new positions effective immediately—in the Greenfield jail."

The crowd cheered as I looked up at Mom and smiled.

It took the mayor a while to get everyone to calm down. Finally, he went on. "Later, I'll speak at length to the press. But for now, let me assure everyone—especially the young people who came out in support of Zoey today—that Zoey is going home."

The mayor looked over to me and Mom and smiled.

"Where she belongs," he said. "And Zoey's cousin, Charlie, will be going to the Los Angeles Zoo, where he can get the attention he needs right now. And where he can be close to his new best friend."

Zoey chose that moment to break from Mom's arms and launch herself at Charlie. The crowd went wild again as the two hugged and kissed happily.

A reporter hurried up to the mayor and handed him a piece of paper. Mayor Powers read it, and I saw his frown of concentration turn into a grin of triumph.

"Ladies and gentlemen," he cried, "please, listen to this. I've just received word that in Los Angeles and several other cities and towns around the country, kids have shown up at their local zoos in support of Zoey and all the other animals here at our zoo."

The mayor's eyes filled with those weird, grown-up "happy tears."

I caught Sloane's eye. "Brad," she mouthed. "Tyler," I mouthed back.

Mayor Powers called for quiet again. "One last thing," he promised, "and then everyone can go back to having fun. None of this would have been possible without the two young ladies on this stage with me. Molly? Sloane?"

Me, the center of attention? You bet! I ran over to join Mayor Powers at the microphone. Sloane and I put our arms around each other and waved to the crowd.

Then I broke away and scooped up Zoey. The day really belonged to her.

I buried my face in her neck and said, "Zoey, I love you!"

Zoey pulled back and with her long, black pointer finger wiped a tear from my cheek. Funny thing—I wasn't the least bit sad.

Chapter 10

"**W**e can't thank you enough, Dr. Miles, Molly." Mayor Powers smiled down at Sloane, who was holding Zoey comfortably in her arms.

"I'm going to miss you, Molly," she said. "It was fun."

I rolled my eyes and laughed. "Yeah, and a few other things, like scary! But I'm going to miss you, too."

"I think our family can squeeze in a trip to Los Angeles later this year," Mayor Powers said.

"We'd love to see you," Mom replied as she took Zoey from Sloane. "And you have to keep us up to date on everything that's happening at the zoo."

"We will," Sloane promised. "Molly and I can e-mail each other every day!"

"Molly, we'd better board now," Mom said.

I gave Sloane one last hug and shook Mayor Powers' hand.

"Oh, Molly," Sloane said as I hefted my travel bag on my shoulder. "Is Brad cute?"

I couldn't help myself. I made a gagging face.

"What about Pete?" I asked.

Sloane blushed. "How did you know?"

I rolled my eyes. "Duh!"

"What about you and Tyler?" Sloane teased.

Now it was my turn to blush.

"So, is Brad cute?"

I thought for a moment. Did I want to share my new best girlfriend with my brother?

I looked at her and grinned. "If you like monkeys."

Once we were in the air and Zoey was occupied with a pad of paper and some colored pencils, I put my head back against the seat and thought about everything that had happened in the past few days.

After the ceremony that turned into a celebration, Mom and I had called home to share the good news with Dad, Brad, and Tyler. But they'd already seen the story on the news and had stories of their own to tell us. With all of us talking at once, it was hard to understand anything except that Zoey was coming home.

Mayor Powers had told us that a brand-new director and assistant director were starting at the zoo immediately. Each had an excellent reputation, and they were already planning to reward the staff who had fought so hard against Ms. Davita and Mr. Sweetbreads. Pete, the elephant trainer, had been given a scholarship so he could start school again in the fall.

The mayor also said that our villains once had been legitimate professionals but that, somewhere along the line, they'd gotten greedy. With the evidence he and the Zoo and Aquarium Association had uncovered—not to mention the evidence the police found in Ms. Davita's and Mr. Sweetbreads' offices and the stuff Sloane and I swore we'd overheard—it looked like they would be spending a long, long time in jail.

We were also told that the police and a big animal rescue operation had already located the snow leopard and a few of the other animals that had been sold to various traveling shows. Arrangements had been made to have the animals transported to good zoos.

I was most excited about Charlie coming to live at the Los Angeles Zoo. I couldn't wait to introduce him to Tyler and Brad. I had the coolest, best friends, I thought. Okay, and a pretty decent brother, too. Brad had called every kid in his class and convinced almost all of them to show up at the Los Angeles Zoo to protest Zoey's transfer.

I guess I must have closed my eyes, because all of a sudden, something made me open them.

You guessed it. Zoey was gone.

I looked across the aisle at Mom. She was snoring.

"Uh, Mom," I said. "Mom?"

"What?" Mom sat up and blinked.

"Uh, Zoey's . . ."

"Oh, no."

"I'll go find her," I said, unbuckling my seatbelt.

It was the high-pitched scream that gave her away. I found Zoey in coach again, this time curled up asleep in the seat of a woman who'd gone to the bathroom.

After apologizing to the hysterical woman and wiping a few orangutan hairs from the cushion—she wouldn't sit down until I did—I led Zoey back to our seats in first class.

Once Zoey was asleep in her own seat, I turned to Mom and sighed.

"This is the last time I travel on a plane with a baby," I said dramatically.

Mom grinned. "'Fraid not," she said.

"What do you mean?" I asked.

"Last night on the phone, Dad told me that Grandpa called. The museum is giving him a big retirement party."

I smiled. "Really? That's great." My grandpa had been the head of the Museum of Natural History in New York for a bazillion years. He was always joking that he was the museum's favorite dinosaur.

"The party is next weekend, and he wants us all to be there," Mom said.

"This is so cool!" I couldn't believe we were going to New York City! Then I frowned. "What does Zoey have to do with Grandpa's party?"

Mom sighed. "Well, there's a minor outbreak of influenza at the zoo. Nothing serious, but it's best if Zoey doesn't visit until the outbreak is over."

I flopped against the back of my chair.

"So she's coming to New York with us," I gulped.

"Exactly," Mom said.

I turned to Zoey.

She opened one eye, looked right at me, and burped.

It was going to be a long, long trip to New York.

I couldn't wait!